Lock Down Publications and Ca$h
Presents

I0658336

CRIME PAYS

Lesson Two
Make It Count

By
Self Made Tay

First Edition 2024

Printed in the United States of America

Lock Down Publications
P.O. Box 944
Stockbridge, GA 30281
www.lockdownpublications.com

Like our page on Facebook: Lock Down Publications
www.facebook.com/lockdownpublications.ldp

Stay Connected with Us!

Text **LOCKDOWN** to 22828 to stay up-to-date with new releases, sneak peaks, contests and more...

Like our page on Facebook:
Lock Down Publications

Join Lock Down Publications/The New Era Reading Group

Visit our website:
www.lockdownpublications.com

Follow us on Instagram:
Lock Down Publications

Email Us: We want to hear from you!

Lesson 1.1
Love Don't Cost A Thing

Shawndra stepped outside to a beautiful shining sun. Which gave a little heat to the last few days of winter, making Valentine's Day just that much more wonderful. She was dressed in upscale casual wear. The smile on her face was radiant. It was as if she was living the dream of her prom that she never had the chance to attend.

Awaiting her at an open limousine door was Derek. She was impressed with his appeal. She expressed it by looking him over twice, following a compliment. "Well, don't you look very handsome." She approached Derek and gave him a kiss on the lips.

"Hey, beautiful." Derek allowed Shawndra to climb into the stretched Cadilac before he followed her in. These past few weeks have been a head-over-heel experience for the two. Confused in their prior relations, they never knew that a love like theirs ever existed. To everyone around them, their love was in question. No one believed for one second that it was something that had just happened. It seemed perfect. Like something that was planned precisely. What was the coincidence that both of their ex's were having an affair, they ended up dead, and then these two are drawn together? Even the homicide detective strongly inquired about the couple's uncommon love. With all the odds stacked against them, Shawndra and Derek had proved, in a short amount of time, that they had a bond that would not be broken.

"So where are we headed, my love?" Shawndra was curious.

"It's a surprise, of course."

Shawndra had freely handed over a lump sum of cash to Derek. She felt as if she owed it to him. Derek took the money and invested it in the first step of his dream. Real estate. He loved his community and was fascinated with building projects. He always wanted to invest in run-down houses and upgrade them into a status of luxury. Now he wanted to pay Shawndra back. Even though the amount was not a match, it was the moment of living the dream that would last forever.

The limo pulled up to the Richmond Convention Center. The driver parked and opened the door, allowing the couple to step out onto the scene. Passers looked on in awe and admiration. Derek took her hand and guided Shawndra to one of the many doors. Before she even entered the building, she could see the red carpet with red rose pedals aligned on each side.

"Oh my God!" Shawndra placed both hands over her mouth trying to suppress her scream. "You really outdid yourself! This is the best Valentines Day Ever! Thank you so much."

"Trust me, it's so small compared to your true worth." Derek was right. Just another small investment for him. Honestly, he felt like the real winner. He had a lady that he knew would kill for him. And even though he was not a killer, he would change that for her. They strolled the carpet in celebrity fashion, and it led them to a table set for two.

Lesson 2.2
Real Recognize Real

"Foster, let's go!"

E had just spent the last three days in the hole. It was a planned fight he paid his opponent to participate in. About ten days ago, CO Crawford was reassigned to another unit in the jail. Not only were their dealings business related, but it was also getting personal. Some days ago, E got word that Crawford was relocated to 4-E. That was one floor lower than the one E was on. It was the floor for high custody felonies which was usually the place E would be housed. Upping his custody level was the only way that he could get downstairs. And he knew exactly how to get it done.

In a matter of minutes, E was out of the hole and down on the fourth floor. He hoped like hell that he would be placed on 4-E, or otherwise he would have to…

"Foster, four E!" the sergeant at the main desk of the floor ordered. In his thoughts he gave thanks and headed towards the tier's door.

Crawford's face lit up with joy. She couldn't hide it even if she tried wanted to. Ten days were too long for her to go without seeing him. Not only had E given her hope financially but intimately. The doors slid open and E walked in. "Hey, Boo," Crawford mouthed only loud enough for his ears to hear. "I missed you." She smiled.

"No bullshit." He dropped his mat and other things at the CO's desk and took a quick observation of the jungle he had entered.

"Down here ain't none like upstairs." That was obvious to E.

"I already know," E confessed.

"I bet you do, with your bad ass." Crawford loved the savage in E. He looked rough now, but not half as rough as he did on the day she met him.

"Aye, E! What's up my nigga?"

E laid eyes on someone he had met a few weeks ago who turned out to be a prominent business partner. "Give me some time right quick. You know I'ma pull up on you," E told Crawford before addressing the man approaching him. "Flex, what's good, big dawg?" The two men dapped up as a sign of respect.

"Shit, maine, I've been trying to hit your people up for the last couple of days. Ain't nobody been givin' me no play." Flex walked E to the back of the triangular shape tier, giving him a hand with his belongings. "I'm up like a whole band on you right now."

"Yeah, I am already hip, fool. You know I'ma straighten that."

"Already, fool. Shidd... dis my cell right here. Ain't no single cells open. I'm quite sure you will be able to finesse your way into one. Til' den though, you can hold dis joint down with me. The phone right beside the cell is my shit. You can hop on that joint whenever. I'ma let the gang know you good and shit. It's a few Mosby niggas on this joint, too. Niggas ain't on shit, to keep it a band, though."

"Already, my nigga. That's real nigga shit." E was very appreciative of Flex welcoming him with open arms along with giving him the rundown of the happenings on the tier. He was almost certain that it was due to the moves that he was making. He did not mind, though, because dealing with a man of Flex's status had its rewards.

E placed his things on the floor where he would be sleeping. He went into his drawers and came out with a bundle of contents. "This the thirty right here for your' band." E handed Flex 30 8-milligram Suboxone strips. "Whenever you make your bread back off that, just let me know. I'ma just put you all the way in position. Let you run point."

"Oh shidd… that's a bet." Flex always grew excited at an opportunity to make some money. He had not too long ago conquered his hunger of greed. It took the death of his brother to get him to that stage. But that did not stop him from using his natural hustler abilities. The past events leading him up to now humbled him, which in turn allowed him to move more strategically. "You the one with the route. However you want to play it, I'm on board."

"Say no more. We gone put this shit together. I got some Za for us, too. We gone blow this shit later. Whenever I get a green light. What's up with you, though? Niggas say you was in the feds." E changed subjects.

"Naw, hell naw." Flex clarified. "them bitches want me, though. they evidence isn't strong enough, though. Bitches don't have any witnesses or none. Plus, I got this boss ass lawyer. Shawty a dawg. She confident that she gone be able to keep it off the federal level."

"Oh yeah?" E was interested in whoever this lawyer lady was that Flex spoke so highly of. "What's shawty's name? I might need to hire her ass. I'm still shopping for a lawyer to help me fight my case."

"Her name Dawn Mornings. You can get your people to look her up. Or I can plug you in with her for real. My name carries a lil' weight with shawty. Shit, mob ties you feel me?"

"Okay, okay. Yeah, I'ma need you to pull some strings for a nigga. I got them bands on deck."

"I'm telling you. Ain't none like investing in your future."

"Ain't it, maine. No bullshit."

Lesson 2.3
Invest

"Damn, shawty! You really won't bull shitting. You got a complete set up in this bitch." That was Tone. Keem's future engineer.

Keem had just finished paying on getting the final additions put into the studio. He invested hundreds of thousands of dollars into its building and patiently waited months for the outcome. Keem wanted Tone to be the first to see the studio. Now both stood in the middle of a fully equipped recording studio. "So, I take it you approve of your' new home?" Keem asked with a slight sense of amusement but was hardly joking.

"Shidd... as long as you got something to eat in dis mother fucker, I'll sit in this bitch all day, everyday." Tone was not playing either.

In fact, it's that same sense of seriousness that led Keem to the idea of investing in Tone. Keem did not have one drop of talent when it came to music. At least not when it came to the creating technique. Although, he was excellent at scouting the potential in someone's creative talent. And of course, he already possessed great management skills. Keem noticed the potential in Tone a long time ago.

Tone used to express his passion and talent for music by beating on upside down buckets on a corner in the Downtown section of the city. The very first thing that Keem noticed about Tone was his rhythmic style of beating the drumsticks. The sounds that caught his ears entered his heart and touched his soul. Right at that moment he wanted to snatch Tone up off that corner and place him in a position that would benefit them both. Unfortunately, the timing was not right. But Keem was sure that the opportunity would present itself. In fact, he planned to make sure it did.

Aside from Tone's ability to put a combination of sounds together, constructing the perfect instrumental. Keem also noticed that the two shared the same love and passion for the art of music. That was the confirmation Keem needed to assure himself that Tone was the right man for the job. Now here they were here. The next step in the process should not even have to be a question.

"I am about to sit in dis bitch and put some shit of banging beats together. The only thing is, we need some niggas that's serious with there hustle and flow. Somebody with fire bars and determined dedication." Tone took the words right off Keem's brain.

"Don't trip off none of that." Keem said. "Trust me, I got that part. You just be ready when they pop up." Honestly, Keem had the slightest idea as to who he could recruit and be willing to invest his money in at the same time. He knew a few niggas that were hot with their lyrics. But he did not think they were worth the paper. Too risky. On the other hand, he knew a few rappers that were dedicated, but the talent just did not reach his personal standards. But as he always does, he planned to figure it out.

"Already, bet." Tone spun around in the chair. "I'm about to start making magic right now. Just let me know what's up. Whenever you ready, you already know where I'ma be."

***

Brick strolled into the Richmond Arts District conference room looking, feeling, and people would've even thought, wearing a million bucks. He was clothed in a dark green

Dolce & Gabbana men's double-breasted, wool-blend tuxedo jacket that was worth almost thirty-four hundred dollars, matched with a pair Dsquared 2 badge applique denim jeans that cost four bands more than his jacket. Just to keep it D&G all the way down, he stepped in a pair of D&G New Tech low top white and dark green sneakers that were surprisingly only half a band. As if, his clothing rounding off close to ten bands was not enough. His jewelry multiplied that cost by ten, at the least. Just his glisten bracelet alone was that of all his clothes put together. "Gentlemen," he spoke as he entered the small conference room that was surrounded by glass walls and doors. He took a seat at the table with his fellow equestrians.

"Brick." Mac greeted, stationed at the head of the table. "Fashionably late as always. You do know we only got dis room for an hour, right?"

"This fool would be late to his own funeral if it was up to him," Dawg stated, adding on to Mac's statement.

Brick looked at his full diamond gold Roman dial Rolex watch with the Jubilee band. The busted down face read five minutes after one PM. "Umm, five minutes late," he said to himself before addressing the room, knowing that they all heard his personal statement. "Well, technically, I really was on time because I pulled up in the parking lot one minute before one hit. Regardless though, excuse my lateness, fellows." He gave a light apology to the group.

"Yeah, it probably was that slow ass stroll that took you so long to get up in here," Black said, adding a little humor to the opening of the conversation. "Don't say none when we start charging your cool as a late fee." The four men broke out in a respectful laugh.

"No bullshit." Dawg was already agreeing to volunteer his vote. "We will get richer faster fuckin' with this nigga. The way his ass be late."

"Now, fellows, there's no need for that. We all know greed is not anywhere in our creed," Brick defended himself.

"Naw. It's not." Dawg agreed again, only this time with Brick. "Time is money. Now that's apart of the creed. Which is you are clearly in violation of."

"Aww shit, sue me already." Brick laughed. The conversation between the gentlemen was completely harmless. In fact, they had these types of joking's quite often. None of them minded it one little bit because they had all proved that when it was time to get down to the business, they all did their parts well and to the tee. If I may add.

The four men present in this room were the Four Horsemen in the city of Richmond. They controlled the drug trade, the street's income, and even most of the crime rate in the city. Little to few people knew about the existence of the square, and the rest would not even believe you if you told them. A lot of people dealt with each of the men in some way, shape, or fashion. Separate they were powerful men who all were able to stand on their own soundly. But together, they were unstoppable. For those that may have known at least two out of the four men, they would compare them to each other. To think that they all were conspiring with each other would blow one's mind out the top of their heads.

"Well, gentlemen, now that we've squandered another five minutes getting to know each other a little more, I'll ask that we get down to business." Mac was the head for the East End of the city which included Mosby Court, the hood he grew up in. They all represented their hoods as the most elite hustlers/criminals from their sections.

"Politics as usual with this fool," Black said harmlessly. "So did you get the information we needed in order to proceed to the next level?" He ended off with a question.

"Actually, I did, but it's not what we've expected," Mac said honestly. "It seems as if we have another hurdle to leap over." Mac tapped a key on the keyboard of his laptop. Subsequently he flipped open a tan folder revealing a number of papers. Before any of the guys fixed their mouths to ask a question, Mac continued with the reasoning of the current meeting. "There is something called a bank charter. We need to apply for it through the OCC, which is the Office of the Comptroller of the Currency— "

"Which is...?" Brick was still confused. Even after Mac gave what he called an explanation.

"Right." Black leveled with Brick as he pulled at his chin hairs with a confused look on his face. "What the fuck is that?" With that, he left two questions up there in the air for Mac to answer.

"If it is cool with y'all, I can continue to interpret the construction of our business at hand. Apparently, we'll have to contact Nicole National Bank to complete the application. And if approved, the wait will still be a hundred and eighty days just to start the construction. Dawg, what's the word on our mule? Did you come up with any associations that we can turn into business partners? You know it's very important that we find a mule to carry this business on their back. This will be way too big to place any of our names on it. It will bring attention that we don't need. But as we discussed, it must be someone that we can trust at least a lil' bit. But, totally control. And that was one of your parts of the mission."

"You already know how I do. Ion play about mine. After scouting my top ten, I have narrowed it down to three and will let the final decision be made by all of us in total."

"As you should," Black stated leaning up in the chair, moving his face closer to the beige manila envelope that Dawg now held in his hands. Dawg was now pulling pictures out of the large envelope. Each one was stapled to a couple pieces of paper. "Damn, my nigga done made profiles for these mother fucker's and some more." Black was impressed, after already being anxious to see who Dawg would bring to the table before he was presented with them.

"Stop playing with a nigga, Black. Like you do not know your boy gets shit done." Dawg looked up at Black while laying the contents of the folder down on the table.

"Already, my nigga. Respect." Black raised a hand up to his forehead, giving his affiliate a respectful salute. "Alright, now, let's see what you working with my nigga."

"Alright, bet." Dawg accepted the challenge. "First, here we have Leilani Johnson," he said separating the first profile from the rest. "She was born and raised in the West End area of Richmond, Virginia where she grew up in a household with her father, a black male named Thomas Johnson, and mother Kailani Johnson, an Asian, who took on her surname from her husband. The moms came to the States landing in New York at the age of two. Spent a decade there before touching down in our hometown of Richmond. While pops, is straight out of the South Side." Respectfully, the men were quiet as they allowed Dawg to give his presentation without any interruptions. "The parents met and fell in love on the campus of VCU where they both went to school. Once they graduated and were done with school, they got married, and started to focus on their careers. The mother is a doctor. Pops was a firefighter. Until he was killed by a fire, running into a house, saving a pair of siblings. Kids survived. Pops died from what they called sudden cardiac death, but everyone knew it was the heavy smoke that did the damage. That was after a twenty-year run of running into fires. Leilani life was set up so perfect that her parents had already put up one point three million dollars in her savings account by the time she was eighteen and able to touch it.

"Leilani was skipped from the tenth grade to the eleventh, allowing her the opportunity to graduate high school at seventeen years old with a GPA of 3.8. Dis women is damn near a genius but is very genuine and so are her intentions. After her four years of studying at VCU, at the top of her class, she moved on to teach preschool for about three years. Her next step was to be a first-grade teacher at George Washington Carver Elementary. There she stayed ten years. Now, she's the boss at Albert H. Hill Middle school after being promoted to principle.

"Aside from that she is also a self-made philanthropist. Does plenty of volunteering work. Feeding the hungry or providing shelter for the homeless. Every year she throws a back-to-school drive that usually turns out just as big as the 2nd Street Festival. She also owns a few non-profit organizations, which is profiting off well, and a couple other businesses that helps her eat. The biggest one being a yoga and meditation spa on the campus of VCU. Shawty lives ducked off somewhere in Windsor Farms, chilling in a one point four-million-dollar home. By herself, aside from two big ass Rottweiler's. Her net worth with assets included and all is six point six million dollars.

"So not only does she have the background and the money, but she also has a community of people who not only believe in her but invest as well. All we have to do is find a way to make her agree. I was thinking—"

"Mac," Black blurted out as if he was just hit with a bright idea. "It got to be brah. I think he will be the perfect one for the job. He's smooth and his self-control is through the roof. I mean, we must go at this woman with something other then money. She already has that. We need to present something that's undeniable."

"Hold up," Brick stepped in. "You don't think you moving a lil' too fast? We still got two other people we must check out."

"Naw, I think she's the one," Mac interrupted with his hand on his chin as if he were in deep thought. "She'll be perfect."

"No bullshit." Black was giving his nod of approval. "Shawty it."

"Yeah, I was thinking' the same," Dawg admitted. "I mean these other two are—"

"Naw, shidd… fuck the other two. The star has been chosen." Brick gave the fourth and final vote needed to elect Miss Leilani Johnson as their business partner/project. "Now, how we gone reel this big fish in?"

"Dawg, give us her daily routine so we can swoop down on our prey the right way on a perfect day," Mac suggested.

"No bullshit, cause this nigga do not play games when it comes to business. My nigga turn professional mode on real quick."

"Alright, so here's the plan…"

Lesson 2.4
Get Money

"The winter almost ova with now," the most prominent grinder on the YNT stated. His name was Bank and his name matched his hustle. YNT stood for Young Niggas Turnt. And that is exactly what they were. "I can't wait for this summer to hit," he said, "I'ma show the fuck off out dis bitch!" Bank held his bankroll in his hand. He flipped it open and started counting. "A nigga done made about three bands out this bitch already." He estimated his number before he was anywhere near done with the count. "And it ain't even three o' clock yet."

"No bullshit." Tru agreed. A comrade of Bank's adding on to the excitement that Bank had brought to the block. "This summer gone be litty!" Tru was E's younger cousin. He was happy as hell to be a part of the team. Little did he know, he had crossed the line of loyalty. Even to the point of no return. Depending on how things would turn out. But for now, to him, things were better than ever for his young life. Sadly, for him though, he was blind and unaware of his disloyalty. A trade that he just might pay his life for.

"I'ma lock to cop me a whip before the summer hit." Another YNT member chipped in who went by the name of Shoota, speaking one of his biggest goals into existence. "Shit gone be something crazy too, watch." Shoota was not what you will truly call a hustler by normal terminology. Although, he was currently connecting with his hustler's ambition, his usual way of collecting funds would be the taker's way. To him, robbing and stealing was faster, easier, and more exciting. Aside from that, Shoota was a walking lethal weapon. A straight fool with the pistol play. At his age, he was the best at gunplay and could even exchange shots with some of the bigger shots in the hood. In fact, hunting his prey for a kill was even more exciting to him than robbery was. On a couple occasions he had murdered his robbery victims just because the taste of blood was just that sweet to him.

"Y'all niggas ain't on shit for real. Niggas ain't gone do shit but get high and trick the bread up on these thirsty ass bitches." Drip expressed his true thoughts. Although he tried to hide it, his words came out a little too bitter for the rest of his peers.

"Damn, Drip," Bank shot back, "hating or naw?"

"No bullshit." Shoota assisted with Bank's question. Even assisting in one of his own. "Nigga gang or naw?"

"Maine, stop playing with me," Drip replied, defending his membership. "Y'all niggas know the count. Matta fact, not only am I gang, nigga I am *gang!*"

"Ain't it, brah." A youngin named Cee sided with Drip. "The fuck wrong with them niggas?" He asked. "Like we ain't been putting in work for this shit, too."

"Ion know what these niggas on. Trying opp a nigga out or some." Drip responded to Cee's inquiry as he reached his hand out to give his longtime friend a dap.

"Naw, I'm just saying," Bank just said, "that sounded like some hating ass shit you jus said brah, like dead ass." Bank verbalized his statement in the form of a joke even with it being far from one.

"Nigga, I ain't hating. For What? I'm getting money with y'all. All I was saying is I hope niggas don't fuck this money up on no dumb shit." Drip either cleared up or covered up his statement. Either way it went, the words did not sound right coming out of his mouth being that he, Cee, and another nigga named Pickle were three niggas from Crieghton Court which was one of the main opposition's to Mosby.

For the life of him, Shoota could not figure out how they ended up on this side of the gang. Regardless of how though, they all played a major part in YNT taking over the Mosby Court Projects. So far, they'd proved their loyalty by the work they had put in. But in the back of Shoota's mind, he just could never forget that their loyalty started with betrayal first.

"Y'all lil' niggas shut the fuck up," BM ordered. With his worst thoughts he would never imagine the stress that came with keeping a gang of young niggas in order. "Ain't nobody doing no hating inside this circle. If I even thought it, that shit would get checked at the gate. Believe that. And ain't any nigga from YNT gone fall off. We ain't having that shit at all either. If a nigga slips and fall, I can promise you he gone lay der and stay der. Nigga, we getting money and dropping our nuts while we at it. Ain't no I in dis team. Everybody has a part to play."

The only truth that did come out of the last lie BM had told was that everyone had a part to play. But most other shit he would just spit was straight bullshit. BM could give two shits about them little fuckers that he bossed around. Maybe except for Shoota. He had a real liking for the minor, but still would not hesitate to throw his ass clean into traffic that was moving through a green light. And as for the rest of his so-called gang, they were only pieces that he needed to place his grand plan into play. To him, which was true, the more money he got, the more money that was his.

Identical twin all black 2023 Range Rover Luxury 7-seater SUVs rounded the corner from Coalter Street, making a right onto Redd Street. The vehicles slowed from their already creeping speed, coming to complete stops, parking next to the curb. The driver door of the first Range Rover popped open and out stepped Maine, the head of Da Fam, sporting an all-black Moncler Billionaire Boys Club hoodie with matching fleece cargo sweat pants. He looked directly at BM and flashed a smile. As soon as his mouth opened it exposed his custom VVS top and bottom clarity natural diamond gold grill. It shined damn near brighter than the sun itself. Just the bling from Maine's teeth pissed BM off. So, the bracelet on his wrist, Gucci frames on his face, rings on his fingers, and an iced-out chain with an angry gorilla face topped with a golden crown on top of his head enraged BM to the point that he wanted to kill.

"What y'all lil' niggas doing out here on my block? Especially, with these opp ass niggas?" Maine asked, posting up on his ride with a gangster lean closer towards the hood. As he did so, the rest of Da Fam was stepping out of both SUVs to post up along with their big dog. The opps he referred to would be the three Crieghton niggas that tagged along with the rest of YNT. At first Maine had slight suspicion that BM was behind the shooting in the APTs not too long ago. Now it was all making plenty of sense and clear to see.

"Maine, go 'head with that shit, nigga." BM started making sure not to display an ounce of fear in front of his soldiers. The hatred BM had for Maine and Da Fam was getting realer by the day. Maine was the runner up, if not the nigga that ran things in the APT and had half of the influence in Mosby. Now that BM was on the hunt to be ruler, he would have to get used to the pressure being applied. Maine was not the one to be pushed over, so taking control would not be an easy task.

"Or what, nigga?" Maine's cousin of the same age asked vexed. He went by Smooth, though the only thing he was smooth about was murder and absconding the scene without a living soul knowing of his sin. "Ya'll lil' niggas know the fucking count out dis bitch." He was already placing his hand near his hip, preparing to clutch. "Or at least mother fucker's better act like they know. Dead ass."

"Nigga ain't trying to hear none of that bullshit!" Shoota stepped up, already clutching his tool. "Niggas know it's a YNT take ova." He took his stance beside BM and could not wait to lift his pistol, take aim at a nigga's head, and blow that bitch clean the fuck off.

"No bullshit." Drip followed suit. He ain't like the fact that he was just referred to as an opposition. Even though he was. And just because he was a part of YNT didn't mean that he all of a sudden had a newfound love for Mosby niggas. In fact, the main reason he agreed to the move was to have a hand in running the vicious Mosby Court Projects. His niggas back around Crieghton just could not wrap their heads around the trade. The shit just did not make no type of sense at all. But Drip did not give a damn. He had a plan himself and felt as if he ain't owe not a soul an explanation. But until his plan unfolded, he was all in with his membership to YNT. "I can't wait to take one of y'all niggas' heads off."

Bank laughed at Drip's comment knowing damn well it was the truth.

"Shidd... what the fuck you waiting on then, pussy?" Maine's other cousin who was just a couple of years older than him asked, whipping out his Glock .40 Gen 4. He was in love with his Glock so much that he named himself after it. Glock. "You need permission from your boyfriend before you make a move?" Glock waived the Glock towards BM, letting it be known that he was attributing him as Drip's boyfriend. Da Fam all shared laughs, cracking up embarrassing Drip, BM, and the rest of the young niggas. "Turnt where? Lil' niggas ain't turnt."

Drip immediately got pissed off at the joke. He pulled his gun out and Cee did the same thing immediately after.

"Ight, y'all niggas better carry y'all ass for my young niggas hop on y'all asses. I ain't gone stop them either." BM advised.

21

"Boo, let us go. These lil' niggas ain't a threat. And they damn sure ain't worth it," the Queen softly pleaded to her husband. She stepped closer to Maine and wrapped her arm around his. Lightly tugging on it, trying to get him to move without being too noticeable.

"Yeah. Y'all niggas chill," Maine ordered his fam. "Do not kill the lil' niggas. They just trying to scrape up some crumbs. Let us finish getting to our business." Da Fam started to load up the car with Maine, Glock, and Smooth being the last few in the car. "Ayee," Maine yelled out back across the street towards BM and YNT. "When y'all lil' niggas ready to get some real money get with me. I might have something left over for y'all lil' niggas. Cuz, I'm telling you, trying to go against the tide gone get your ass drowned."

"Maine, get your ass in his car," Queen shouted from the passenger seat through the window.

The whole time Maine was talking, Smooth held a huge amount of cash in his hand flashing it, tantalizing YNT making them wish that their bank was even close to as big as his. Soon though, they were all packed into the SUV's and were pulling away from the curb. "Get you some money, lil' nigga!" Smooth yelled out the window as they dipped.

"I can't fuckin' stand them bitch ass niggas, brah, like dead ass!" Shoota was inflamed with anger. "When you gone let us get at them bitch niggas again, BM? We got to slide on that shit."

"Calm your ass down, nigga," was BM's reply. "You never let a nigga get you out your bag so bad that you lose focus on the mission. Which for us is the money, nigga. And plus, they got to feel our presence some type of way because at first them niggas never paid us no mind at all. We got their attention now. So, just stay down. And when it is time to turn up, just make sure you mother fuckers ready. We gone have our day, but on our time. Right now, though it's grind time."

Lesson 2.5
Intelligence Over Emotions

Lil' One sat zoned out on a stack of bricks around his hood in Hillside Court, located in the South Side of Richmond, Virginia. The only two things that consistently crossed his mind was the murder of his best friend Crow and a way to get back at his killer. Lil' One and Crow were paid by Keem, who was paid by Mac, to keep eyes on BM. After slipping one too many times, Lil' One and Crow were caught down bad. Left exposed, wide open for BM snatch their souls like the grim reapers in Born in the Grave. Lil' One survived the attack. Something that his sidekick wasn't able to do. Now Lil' One spent his everyday existence contemplating on a way to even the score with BM. The only thing he had going in his favor though was that BM was confident that he had left both victims dead in that car that day parked on Mosby Street. That confidence, along with his deadly focus of taking over Mosby Court Projects, which was one hell of a task within itself, distracted BM from doing the actual homework of making sure of their deaths.

Though BM had struck him several times, other than the bullet wounds, all Lil' One walked away with after healing was a limp. There was a small fracture in his ball and socket bones from the bullet that tapped his hip. Really though all he cared for was his brain and his trigger fingers. If the three of them were functional he would put his life on the cross in exchange for BM's. The only thing was how? Lil' One witnessed the cleverness of BM up close and personal. Even before then, he had already heard of the murder game that BM was known to lay down. Plus, through word of mouth, Lil' One had heard about BM's recent whereabouts. How he had assembled a tight knit army together and that he was aiming at the King of the Hill crown. Now knowing that BM was not alone only made it harder for Lil' One to construct a plan.

"Lil' One, what's up, fool? You good?" A few teenagers around the same age as Lil' One was in stride, heading his way. "You been moving like a zombie out this bitch for the past few days, my nigga. You gone shake back soon."

"Shidd... I'm surprised his ass ain't crashed out yet," another one of the few said, adding in. "You know that Crow shit got my nigga tight."

"Yeah, I know," the first one replied. "But shidd... Crow was my dawg too but—"

"Naw, that count was different when it came to Crow and Lil' One." A third one threw in two more cents. "Them niggas was tight like rubber bands on a ponytail. Dead ass though, Lil' One, you alright?" Lil' One was as quiet as a Buddhist meditation practice. "Ayee, this nigga gone, shawty, dead ass."

"No bullshit. I hope his ass ain't smoking them rocks." The teenager that opened the conversation from the beginning spoke again.

"Shidd... I will be fucked up, too. Especially after I just lost my day one nigga right at the time we was deep in our bags. That shit got to hurt. Ayee, Lil' One, I know you hear me fool." He spoke to Lil' One as if he were in the state of a coma or something. "Whenever you ready to go on that Mosby shit just let me know, my nigga. I'm on go, dead ass."

Lil' One heard every word that was being said from his peers. It was just that nothing they were saying gave him any bright ideas at all.

"Speaking of them Mosby niggas," the initiating talkative young one took control of the conversation again. "Word on the street is that BM out that bitch getting to that money like crazy-crazy."

"Yeah, I heard."

"Man, they say that nigga recruiting Creighton niggas and some shit on his team. Shidd… if he is letting them niggas slide in, I know a nigga like me can get in where he fit in."

"Nigga, we over here talking about getting at them nigga's and you sitting right here talking about getting with them nigga's."

"Shidd… everybody else slimed out, why the fuck—"

And that's when it hit him. Lil' One stood straight up, walking off, leaving the rest of them to continue discussing their bullshit. The first step to his plan had just been formulated in his head.

"Lil' One… Lil' One… that nigga burnt out for real." The insignificant words bounced off the back of Lil' One while a strategy bounced all through his mind.

Lesson 2.6
Pick Your Poison...

Derek stepped out of his apartment on Ambrose Street and headed towards his car. The sun shined, heating the Richmond city air up to a warming 59-degrees. Derek was dressed in his DTLR work uniform, on his way to his job that he loved so much. Stepping into the street he walked around his car, approaching the driver's door of his vehicle.

"Aye, nigga!" A man called out towards Derek, getting out of a car of his own from the opposite side of the same street. Derek looked over but paid the man little to no mind, looking away to place his focus on unlocking his car's door. "Yeah, you, nigga!" The man continued to press on, clearly making his way towards Derek.

"Boo! Who is that?" Shawndra put it into question just catching the encounter as she was coming out of the apartment herself. She locked the front door and headed down the four flights of stairs, coming off the small concrete porch.

"Ion know dude." Derek returned the answer. "That nigga can't be talking to me."

Oh, but he most definitely was. The man was big and brawny, built like a professional body builder. Though Derek's answer was true, the man knew exactly who he was. "Word on the street is nigga that you got my baby mama killed."

The words that flew off the man's tongue completely overwhelmed the thoughts of Derek. He knew that Kimberly's baby boy was not his. Yet he still cared for him as if he were. The thing he was surely unsure of though was exactly who her baby's father was. Derek had suspected a couple guys in mind, but this man was never one of them. In fact, he never even knew that this man had existence on earth at all. That also devastated him at the thought of this man having knowledge of his seed, yet leaving him in the care of another man. Derek did not have any kids. So, he could not really relate. Yet still, if he did, he would have never had the thought of abandoning his child.

This whole situation was confusing to Derek altogether. One of the biggest reasons was how the fuck did this nigga know about him setting Kimberly up? It had to have just been a speculation because no one really knew for sure aside from Shawndra, Kadesha who was Shawndra's best friend and physically her partner in crime, and himself. He was about ninety-five percent sure that none of them had run their mouths about their secret. "Maine, Ion know what the fuck you talking about, brah. I don't have shit to do with Kim getting killed. Nigga, that was my girl. What the fuck I look like killing her?" Derek did an okay job at lying. But a true con-artist would be able to see right through that shit. "Plus, nigga, who the fuck is you any-fuckin'-way?" Derek asked two good ass questions back-to-back. Unfortunately, though, for Derek, dude was not trying to hear that shit at all.

"Nigga, I'm not trying' to hear that shit." He verbalized while simultaneously taking a full heavy swing, aiming at Derek's open face with a balled-up fist.

The surprising blow pushed Derek back towards the body of his own car. Had it not been there, Derek's body was more than likely to find his way to the ground.

"Boo! Watch out!" Shawndra screamed but it was too late. By the time Derek had heard Shawndra's voice, it was drowned out by the smacking sound of the unknown's man fist connecting to Derek's face, along with the ringing of his ear drum. Now fighting against two attacking heavy weight championship boxing fists and gravity, Derek struggled to find his way back up to his balancing feet. "Get your ass up, Derek!" Shawndra motivated her man as she rushed to his side in a hurry.

Derek balled his head into his arms, allowing him to block a couple of blows. Right after doing so, he pushed at the man's torso with as much strength as he could muster now. The man took two steps backwards and Derek proceeded to stand his ground, squaring up, preparing for battle.

Now the two men stood face to face. They both used that moment to get a quick read of each other by staring in the opponent's eyes. Derek's energy gave off a lack of confidence but fearless, nonetheless. The opposition loved that. He smirked an unethical smile as he thought of how he would use Derek's emotions to defeat him. The look in the man's eyes was malignant. If he could not kill Derek with his bare hands, then he wanted to at least break an arm bone or something. Maybe his nose. Whatever the case may be, the man had the full intent to cause harm to Derek regardless.

He was not sure if Derek had anything to do with the mother of his child Kimberly getting murdered. True indeed he had heard of his suspicion. Especially since everyone was talking about how Shawndra and Derek got together right after both of their partners were murdered together. The signs were just too clear. It was like hiding in plain sight. But the evidence was none. It was one of those things where everyone knew it for sure but could not prove it or just did not give a fuck. Honestly, he did not even give two shits. Barely even noticed the bitch was gone. This nigga was the type of nigga that hoped and even advised that Kimberly stayed with Derek. That way he would not have to deal with the baby nor her ass. The only thing that was good about Kimberly in his mind was the pussy and the price. The bitch just loved fucking, and would do so for something as little as a blunt.

So, this commotion that took place at the time really had nothing to do with Kimberly resting in peace. The thing that truly angered this man was the fact that Kimberly was gone. In addition to that, so was her mother. And her father was a nobody ass junky running around in the streets. The nigga might as well had been dead alongside the other two. With that being said, the bastard baby boy was forced onto his side of the family. The DNA came back matching the blood of his own. He had already known that. But now it pissed him the fuck off that his family and everybody else now knew as well. Now, here he was, mad at Derek because he felt as if Derek should have been a real man and taken the baby in as his own. He thought of Derek as weak, a pussy, and a bitch for abandoning the baby. To defend Derek, he did have those thoughts to keep the baby at first. Shawndra and him even had talks and debates on whether they should or not. At the end, Derek decided against it. He had just wanted to be rid of Kimberly and everything that had anything to do with her. Besides, he also did not think that he would be ready to go against a whole family who he just knew would come for the child. Never in a thousand years would he think that he was being targeted for not wanting to keep another's man baby.

"You bitch ass nigga!" Shawndra screamed at the top of her lungs. Derek wished he could have stopped her but she had already snuck up close enough to catch her target straight Z'd. That was sleep, that is. Shawndra belabored the man over the head with her all-black Tory Burch Ella patent tote bag. The contents in the bag were heavy enough to cause an arduous injury to the man's face. "Yeah, bitch!" Shawndra continued in pursuit of her attack. "Get your bitch ass off my man!"

Not only was his head throbbing form the strike, but now he had been called two too many bitches. With his right hand clutching the right side of his face, the man spun around as swift as a Michael Jackson spin, landing a clean open palm slap to the side of her face. The counterattack not only awed her but humbled her as well. Fast. Her body damn near crashed on top of the hood of the car from the powerful blow.

All the pain in Derek's body could not have given him the strength he had just received from seeing a man lay hands on the same woman that had killed for him. Derek was immediately impassioned with a melodramatic animosity. So much so that he forcefully catapulted towards the man like a firing cannon ball. Throwing his fist back-to-back as if they were projectiles being spat out of an automatic weapon. The blows landed to the eye, temple, lip, and jaw, doing as much damage as Derek could engine up at the time. For the man we now knew as Kimberly's baby's daddy, all the barrages did for him was distract him from a continuous beating on Shawndra, while also pissing him off even more than his miserable life already had. Already mad as a leader of the Ku Klux Klan that had found out his daughter was pregnant by a street nigga. Adding to the release of epinephrine in his body which caused his adrenaline to rush like an NFL sack leader that needed one more sack to break the record. Kimberly's baby's daddy was numb to all the pain enduring it all like a drugged ICU patient. He took two more punches to his face. Eating them as if knuckle sandwiches were truly an edible item.

Surging towards Derek with both of his hands held high seeking to be wrapped around Derek's neck, the man released an angry growl that closely imitating a guarding dog. "I'ma kill your stupid ass! You dumb ass nigga!" Kimberly's baby's daddy scowled, finally catching hold of Derek's neck, now trying to choke the life out of him.

"Let him the fuck go!" Shawndra pleaded, grabbing at the man's arm, trying to loosen up the grip he had on Derek.

He shook her off as easily as dropping a wrapped towel from around his waist. With a backwards kick he banged his foot into the top of Shawndra's knee. The pain caused her to

CRIME PAYS 2 | SELF MADE TAY

buckle down to the ground while crying out in pain. Derek, trying to fight back, kneed the man in his groan area, trying to aim directly at his nut sack.

"Aww, bitch!" The man verbally reacted. His physical reaction was worse. It started with a head-butt to the bridge of his nose. Blood immediately rushed out of Derek's nostrils covering his mouth and chin like red paint on a canvas. Next, the man smacked Derek up the side of his head before banging it up against the side of the car. "I'ma knock some sense into your dumb ass," the man said as he banged Derek's head up against his own vehicle once more. Derek then raised a hand to strike his attacker. The man simply knocked Derek's hand out of the air like an attempted murder on a fly. Now trying to lift the opposite hand, Derek took a shot at another strike. "Oh, you trying to fight back, pussy?" Kimberly's baby's father asked an obvious question. Just that fact made him madder. He went to wrap both of his arms around Derek's head. He wanted to cuff it like a football and squeeze it like a lemon.

With motion that was swifter than a current of electricity, Derek ducked the broad arms and side stepped out of the tight space. Now Kimberly's son's dad was the one stuck in between the car. Derek continued to think rapidly. With a full tilt he hooked left, right, left, right, right, not even thinking about giving the biggest between the two a chance to bounce back. All the blows were connected to the man's jaws and cheek bone. Next, Derek put the man in a headlock and applied as much pressure as he could muster. Tightening his arms in hope that the man's— who was just visiting to cause harm— head would pop open like a gusher. Derek did not plan to let go until it did. Not too much time had passed by but to Derek it seemed like forever. It was a more likely chance that Jesus would be back before Derek would be able to explode this man's brains out of his head with just his bare hands. Unfortunately for Derek but obviously, it never happened.

31

What did happen though was unexpected. Completely giving up on attempting to remove Derek's tight grip from around his neck, which only gave more strain to the struggle, the man reached back as far as he could and waved his hands around with a wiggle of his fingers in search for Derek's face. Once he laid hands on Derek's face, the man used both of his thumbs, sticking them directly into Derek's eyeballs. The act caused Derek to scream, simultaneously releasing the hold on his predator. And that's when things went back downhill. The man turned around quicker than a Beyblade. He gave Derek a stinging uppercut the way Deebo did Red on *Friday*, with a little less exaggeration. Derek wobbled to the ground like a slice of baloney on its way to the kitchen floor. From there he was kicked and stomped. The best thing for him to do was to ball up in the fetus position.

Suddenly, gunfire had echoed through the Whitcomb Court Projects. At once the man looked up to see exactly where the shots had come from. There were three men standing on the curb right across the street, starring him down.

"I'on know what y'all got going on," the one standing slightly ahead the other two started, "but this shit over with. Nigga, you ain't even from round this bitch. Get the fuck up off my homeboy 'for you end up with some unexpected problems."

Looking down at Derek made it be known. "You lucky them niggas saved you just now. Oh, but I'ma catch your ass again for sure." He left Derek with a promising threat before calmly heading over to his car. On his way, he made sure to lock his eyes on the three-deep mob. One of them mumbled something that was hard for him to hear. Instead of starting up a conversation, the man just chuckled after spreading a smirk across his face.

Shawndra rushed over to Derek's side. She kneeled to the ground and helped him lift his upper body from it. "You okay, baby?" she asked, deeply concerned, observing all the injuries that were visible. And even double-checking for any that may have been out of sight. "That bitch ass nigga," she uttered with a heart full of hatred that she usually never sensed. She looked over her left shoulder to witness the man climb into his car. "Who the fuck is that anyway, Boo?" While asking the second question, Shawndra locked her eyes in on the man's license plate number. Using her photographic memory, she then locked the numbers into the safe in her brain. "TPA—" she mumbled to herself, turning her head back around to face Derek.

"What?" Derek asked, confused. His head was throbbing along with a few other areas on his body. The questions Shawndra asked back-to-back were left unanswered, twisted his brain. Now even more with her mumbling made it hard to understand her words. "What you say?" He asked again just for assurance. "I told you Ion know that nigga. And yeah, I am alright." While Derek piled himself out the middle of the street, Shawndra helped him out, pulling him up by his arm. "At lease I'ma be alright. I am hurting like a motherfucker right now, but it is bearable." He assured Shawndra of the truth. To be honest, Derek was not a street nigga by any means at all. And although he was not a gangster, he was not a bitch by a long shot neither. "Aye, good looking out, fellows." Derek nodded and gave his respectful salute to the troops that had just shortened his ass whooping.

"Already, D. You good?" one of them asked to speak for them all.

"Yeah, I am good, brah. I appreciate y'all niggas. Real shit."

"Say no more, brah," they advised him and stood there until they were for sure that Derek was safe.

"You still going to work like dis?" Shawndra asked worried, hoping he would wisely call out for once, seeing that this was an urgent matter that required heavy attention.

"I really don't think you should." She presented her honest advice.

"Ion know. I do want to go. But if you advise against it, I will listen to you."

"Yeah, I'ma call out with you so we can go down to the hospital to make sure that you are completely okay. Then afterwards, we can come back home and rest for the rest of the day and may even tomorrow if we need to."

"Alright, babe, that is a bet. You are driving, though."

They took their time getting into the car, and soon Shawndra was slowly pulling off from the curb. For a lengthy moment, the ride was awkwardly quiet. The only thing that gave off sound was the radio that hummed at an incredibly low frequency. "Thank you for taking up for me, Boo." Shawndra broke the silence.

Truth be told Derek, felt a little ashamed. "Shit, I should be thanking your ass for real." He expressed the truth. "Ion know if—"

"No, Boo, stop it." Shawndra stopped Derek mid-sentence. "I saw the way you got once that nigga put his hands on me. It seemed like you had more willpower to defend me than you did yourself. And I thank you for that. When it came to my protection, your ass did not play any fucking games. And to let you in on a little secret, that is all a woman wants in her man— is to know that he would protect her at all cost. So, with that, I want to thank you from the bottom of my heart. I love you."

"I love you, too," was all Derek said, just leaving it at that. The rest of the short ride was enjoyed with lovely thoughts of the love and affection he felt from Shawndra while listening to the words of Ella Mai's *DFMU*.

***

"Naw, hold up, nigga, don't touch them dice!" A themand was shouted from a nigga who held bank in a three-dice game of Celo. His back was facing the wall in the back of the triangular shaped tier in the jail. "You ain't even have no money down. What you think you about to shoot for?" The dreads on his head swung from side to side as he bopped, animatedly expressing his words. Most of the floor in their area was covered with fish pouches, packages of beef, noodle packs, Honey Buns, cookies, and other types of snacks. The dice game was one-sided as the banksman threw hits as if he had complete control over the dice.

"Maine, that's crazy how that nigga did Thug." A gang of men crowded around the flat scene hanging on the wall. The virtual image was a video of Young Thug for his latest song *From A Man*. "Nigga done told them people they were a gang and some more shit!" Yelling over the television, the gangster closest to it stood with a brush in hand stroking his waves. "They gone clap his ass when he hit them streets, dead ass." The Gang members surrounding him all passed around an infectious laughter. "Naw, no bullshit though. I know the money already on that nigga top by now. Shit, I will take that motherfucker for the low. Fifteen, twenty bands right now, and max a nigga out with two bags full of commissary. That shit gone take a nigga out the door," he added, joining in on the laugh with the rest of the gang.

"Omaha, fellows. Y'all know what it is," Flex said as began to shuffle the cards in his hand. The table full of poker players released a stressful sigh. That was Flex's favorite game. He always bet big and he rarely lost. Ever. "Go ahead somewhere with that crybaby ass shit, gang. Dead ass. Y'all niggas better step y'all game up. Maybe if y'all stop competing against each other and focus on me. Then somebody other than me can win. But until then…" Flex hunched his shoulders before extending his arms to deal the deck of cards.

These were the main events going on down in the jail. Specifically, on 4-E. Behind the Poker table was the spades table where they did have games going on for a ridiculously small wager. Usually, it would not go over a dollar a man. The phones were full, a few niggas were working out, and a couple groups hurdled the wall.

Continuing all the way through the tier is where you were able to locate C.O. Crawford and E. They stood at the CO's desk which was shaped like a horseshoe, so that is what they called it. "You been really popping since you got your little Ghana braids in a bun. I cannot keep my eyes off your ass. Every time you step back on the tier my eyes be locked in."

Crawford blushed heavily through her caramel complexion cheeks. "Thank you, Boo," she replied. The feelings she had inside of her were inexpressible. I mean true indeed, it was the exact same thing that she dreamed of. These feelings were everything she had ever wanted. But to obtain them seemed unreal. So much so that she was left speechless about them. But then again, she never minded it. She would much rather melt in her wonderful feelings while expressing the love she had for E. And besides, there were much bigger things to discuss anyhow. "But look, though," Crawford stated making sure she had E's full attention. "I found out why they moved me down here to the fourth floor."

"Oh, yeah?" E was listening carefully. He even checked around him to make sure there was no one else trying to catch on to his words by eavesdropping. "Shit, already know you got to put me on game. Who is the little birdie?"

Crawford laughed at E's question for a couple reasons. For one, it was funny to her and secondly, she was smart enough to play the seriousness of their conversation off. "Duhh…" She began. "What you think I said something for?" She returned the question with one of her own before continuing. "You remember that boy who had got splashed with that hot water from the microwave then they jumped him?" Once Crawford's third question rolled off her tongue, E then started from there to process it. From the look on his face, Crawford could conclude that he was confused. So, she decided to help him out a little further along. "The one that was saying he was from South Side. But the Creighton niggas put him out there and said that he had gotten ran from over Fairfield Court, I think, or something like that. No?" Crawford had a slightly confused look on her face trying to make sure that she was staying on track with her story.

E's eyelids jumped open wide a little. Enough for Crawford to know that he was catching on to something she said. E rotated his head slightly right about sixty-six degrees in that direction to be exact. Once he found who he was looking for, E locked eyes on his target. The man had no idea that he had become an enemy of E's suddenly. Not even a single worry.

"Exactly," Crawford said, giving confirmation. "That one right there. The other COs have been talking about that nigga. Saying how he is a jailhouse snitch and shit. And check this out." Crawford was pulling up something on her computer screen. She turned it around so E would be able to get a better view. "Don't none of they asses like the motherfucker because not only is his ass a rat, but he also is a fucking child molester."

But when E read the child molesting charges in addition to a handful of other bullshit in the man's records, it made him stand straight up. His emotions were angered, and his face expressed it.

"No, wait!" Crawford themanded, reaching out to place a hand on his arm in case she would have to pull him back. "Do not do nothing stupid, E'vel. For one, you are too smart to be moving reckless like that. I know you mad as a bitch, but take the foul so you can get a one deal. You feel me?" she asked him to look into his eyes for an answer. No words from E. His agreement came in the form of a nod. Crawford relaxed a little more when she saw E settling down some. "Thank you." She showed her appreciation to E for him taking the humble road. "Besides, Boo, you cannot be the one to do it anyway. It is gone fuck up everything we have started."

Crawford was completely right, and E agreed with it every step of the way. Regardless though, he knew that the nigga would have to get dealt with in a drastic measure and soon. There was no way possible that E would even be able to sit around for long knowing what he had on the future victim. He knew for damn sure that when his cell mate got word of the situation he would feel the same, if not more outraged. He strolled over to Flex and in front of the whole table, in the middle of the game, dropped a bug in his ear that no one else was able to catch. In E's mind the news could not wait.

Flex looked up from the cards in his hands in a sullen state and laid his eyes on the topic of their conversation. His mind was running like an Olympic medalist trying to visualize the perfect plan to punish the weak soul whom he felt had no right to live. "Say no more," Flex assured E aloud. "We gone manage that shit with ease." Now others at the table were looking around trying to catch on to exactly what it was that Flex was speaking of. "Check," he simply said, leaving them all in the dark and placing his focus back on the card game at hand. "Build that pot up for me."

***

"Yeah, alright, that is a bet. I appreciate you, big dog." Shy handed out some energy of gratitude looking over his car. He was currently at Leete Tire & Auto Center on Commerce Road. The objective was to get a set of brand-new tires on his truck. Now that the mission was complete and he was satisfied as he always was when coming here, he was now ready to leave. As he opened the door to his vehicle, he heard another car door slam shut. At first, he really paid the noise no mind. That was until he heard a voice.

CRIME PAYS 2 | SELF MADE TAY

"Hey, excuse me." A woman's voice vibrated through the air waves, catching Shy's ear drums. From the beginning her voice was as sweet as honey.

Shy turned around and came face to face with one of God's most beautiful creatures he had ever had the chance to see. Surely enough, he had seen beautiful women here and there. Most of them were taken and the ones that were not had some type of issue that he was just not willing to deal with. Guess beauty just was not enough for him. Then, there were some women he knew that were rich in character and morals but had poor beauty habits. Some of them just did not take their appearance as seriously as their brains or money. Shy thought that nothing was wrong with that at all. He respected the women who put certain priorities first. Though he still could understand a woman who would exclude her beauty. To him, women had a beauty that could not be matched by any other creature on the earth.

"Hey, can you show me how to get to Hillside, please?" But this woman's beauty was so heavenly that it hypnotized Shy. "Umm... hello?" the woman said waving a hand in the air, trying to regain his attention.

"Huh? Oh, damn. My bad," Shy uttered, feeling only a little shy. He snapped back to reality, coming back down to earth. "Yeah, what you say again?"

"Hillside. Do you know how to get there? I guess my GPS messing up because it says that I am here, but I highly doubt that this is it," the heaven-sent woman explained again with clarity. She was hardly offended, nor did she judge Shy for his moment of mental absence. She would catch that same look at least once a week from some stranger out in the world.

For Shy though, a moment assuring as this one was rare. He never froze up in the presence of a beautiful woman. It usually gave him more confidence. But this one was different. She sported a cream knitted turtleneck sweater dress with a long midi slit and long bell sleeves, with a pair of Michael Kors culver embellished nubuck and glitter chain mesh lace-up boots. Shy figured the boots alone had to be worth almost three-hundred dollars. He was intrigued by her style. She coordinated herself in a way that was foreign to Shy.

"Oh, yeah, it is right here. Basically." Shy assured her. "You missed the street to turn on. That shit happens sometimes, though. All you gotta do is go back down Commerce and make the right on Bruce Street." Now that Shy thought about it, he grew a little confused. "I know damn well you do not live out there. For one, because I ain't never seen you out there before. And for two, you are too…" Shy never finished what he wanted to say though it rang loud and clear in his head.

"No, I'm not even from here at all. I am from Alexandria, Virginia to be exact."

"Oh, yeah?" Shy asked, now even more curious. He closed his car door and headed closer to her car. "NVA, huh," he asked but really making a statement. "So, what's your name?" He now asked a legitimate question. "I'm Shy, by the way," he greeted before she was able to say her name.

"Okay, Shy." The words came out slightly slow. "That is a little different," she admitted. "I like it, though, because I love different things. And my name is Destiny." She introduced herself placing an open palm over her breast as a gesture to indicate herself. "This is honestly my first time in Richmond. I came down to visit my favorite cousin who just moved down here not too long ago."

"Well, Destiny," Shy had finally made it around the car now standing face to face with Destiny and close enough to stick his arm out for a handshake. "Welcome to the City of Richmond. I hope you have a wonderful experience while you are here."

Destiny blushed with a little giggle as she accepted Shy's handshake. She giggled a little more when Shy raised her hand up to his lips, placing a kiss on the back of her hand.

"Well, I must say that it is starting off a little enjoyable." Destiny admitted. "Now, would you be able to assist me to my destination?"

Shy lowered the lovely young lady's hand and released it. He then let out a little laugh as if he was lightly amused by the encounter. "Look at me," he said aloud but just talking to himself. "Helping Destiny to her destination. I must be moving up in this world, huh?" He never expected the question to be returned with an answer. "What street your people live on?" He directed the last question directly to Destiny.

"1409 Minefee Street. She said it was across the street from the projects of Hillside Court. To just go a little way down the street and her house would be the first one on the right after passing a few apartments. But I cannot even get to Hillside to—"

"Hop in your car and follow behind me. I will get you to where you need to be. I know exactly where it is." As Shy was giving the instructions, he was also heading to his car. He pulled his car door open again and jumped into the truck. As soon as the engine came to life, the tumultuous music started to boom through the speakers. The song was *All My Life* by Lil' Durk featuring J. Cole. Shy could not get enough of it. It was mandatory that he heard it at least a few times a day. Every time he heard the song it felt like the first time again. It was just that type of song for him.

Instead of being a typical nigga like a normal street nigga would be, Shy did his best to avoid as many projects as he could. It was not too hard to say that Destiny was far from a product of the streets. Probably never even had any experience with the hood at all. And Shy loved the fact that she was not one who tried to function as if she was hood, knowing damn well that she was anything but that. Shy respected that and decided to take her down the road less traveled, going around the projects instead of smack dead in the middle of it.

Still though, Destiny was able to witness the buildings, hustlers, addicts, the kids running all over, and the whole nine yards. It really sent her through a wave of mixed emotions. She felt scared, anxious, nervous, surprised, confused, sorrowful, and surprisingly for some reason proud. Finally, they were pulling up to a little three-bedroom white house with a bright red door and window shutters. As soon as the cars were geared in park, the door to the house was flying open.

"Hey, Cousin!" A young lady that looked to be in her young twenties came strutting down her short sidewalk with her arms already spread out wide.

"Hey, Cousin!" Destiny shouted back as she jumped out of her car and ran around it.

When the women met up with each other, they fully accepted one another by wrapping their arms around them. From there they warmly cuddled in each other's embrace.

A tear from all the happiness even rolled down Destiny's face. She made no attempt to stop it. "Oh my God, baby, I miss you soooo much!" Destiny expressed while the two of them rocked side to side on their feet.

Even though Shy's deed was done, he still decided to stick around. It was something about the connection that the cousins had made that sparked a light in his soul. It was rarely witnessed by him. So, he used this moment to look at what real love looked like. Stepping out of his whip, he walked around to the other side of the car and leaned up against the passenger side of it. Shy suddenly noticed Destiny's cousin's eyes fall upon his presence.

"And, Cousin, who is this?"

Shy looked around slightly left and right as if he was looking for someone else to be there. But he knew certainly that that was not the truth. Now, for the second time, he felt a little uncomfortable.

"Oh," Destiny spoke up. "His name is Shy. I was lost and he helped me get back on track."

"Yeah, I was just showing her where you lived and shit like that. Making sure she was good out here." Shy spoke on his own behalf, doing a wonderful job of covering up his uncomfortableness.

"Well, I am glad you did because I was about to come out there and look for her. So, thank you so very much, Mr. Shy."

"Naw, you good. Shawty cool as I'on know what. I did not mind at all. It was my pleasure. Now that I see she good, I feel a lot better. But for some reason I cannot allow myself to leave without asking to see you again." The ladies quickly looked at each other, flashing smiles brighter than a pair of flashlights. "I mean at least before you leave the city again, or whatever."

"Girl, it sounds like you got a date already."

"No, Jo-Jo. Don't do that—" Destiny had tried to stop her Cousin from talking. Then at that same time, Shy stopped her words in mid-sentence.

"Don't do what?" Shy jumped in directing his comment towards Destiny. "That's exactly what I'm trying do." The confidence that Shy presented was incredibly attractive to both ladies.

"It's a date!" Destiny's cousin, who Shy figured her name to be Jo-Jo stamped it as if it wasn't up for debate.

"What? A date?" Destiny simply asked.

"Yes," Jo-Jo replied. "Shy, you, Carter, and me. It is a double date. Did you two exchange numbers yet, Shy?" She swung her question around to him.

"Umm, naw," Shy said. He was already pulling his phone out. "What's the number?"

Jo-Jo spat the number out like a threatened snake would do its venom. Destiny just stood there and allowed the exchange to go down without any further protest.

"Alright bet. I am most definitely gone hit y'all line." Shy stood up from his vehicle. He started to turn around and head into the street. But before he did, he stopped and asked. "And what's your name?" Shy wanted to make sure that he had the right name and that was what she preferred to go by.

"My name is Josephine, but everybody calls me Jo or Jo-Jo. You can call me Jo because nobody calls me Jo-Jo except my mama and fav-o-rite cousin." She looked towards Destiny letting it be known that she was that favorite cousin of which she was speaking.

"Ight bet," Shy said now, opening his car door. "Ya will take care of each other. Nice to meet you, Jo and I will see you again soon Destiny. It was meant to be." Shy dropped a little game that caused Destiny to shine with her smile as she watched him roll down the street and turn away.

Lesson 2.7
...Or Die

Shawndra sat waiting behind a dumpster that was surrounded by a wooden fence. The dumpster was for the use of the occupants in the Ashley Oaks Apartments located in the Fulton section of Richmond, Virginia. She was dressed in all black head to toe. Not an inch of her skin was exposed except for the skin above her nose and the little that surrounded her eyes and eyebrows. She waited anxiously with great patience. To be exact, it had now been two hours forty-six minutes and thirty-six seconds and counting.

At three twenty-five in the morning, the person she waited for had finally stepped out of the back of an apartment building. Staggering to his car the man was drunk as a wino that posted in the front of a corner store. He spoke though the receiver of the phone that was placed to his ear. His words were loud and flirtatious.

"Bitch you know I am about to tear that pussy up. I have been waiting for you to hit me up all night. Dead ass."

His walk was wobbly. It was a struggle for him to maintain his balance. It all played perfectly into Shawndra's plan. She crept from around the fence that surrounded the garbage can. She already had her handheld accessory held up high at face level to her targets face. "Drop the motherfucking phone bitch! Now!" Shawndra themanded angrily. As soon as she realized the target hesitated, she dropped the level of the gun and aimed it at his feet, applying pressure to the trigger. The gun went off as a bullet flew out of the gun. It struck the middle of the target's right foot making him drop the phone unintentionally. From there, Shawndra ran up on him as smooth and fast as she could while swinging the pistol in her hand, clashing it up against his face with a passion of brutality. "Next time I tell your ass to do something bitch, your ass better do it." Shawndra affirmed. "Now get on your fucking knees, right now!" She themanded another themand.

"Alright, bitch! Alright. I got you," he vocalized as he made his way to the ground, one knee at a time with his hands held high into the air as if he was being apprehended by a police officer.

"Watch your fucking mouth when you talking to a boss bitch," Shawndra ordered as she placed the gun upside his head once again. "Matter fact it is Boss Bitch to you. You little hoe." She concluded. "Now look me in my motherfucking face," she ordered. He did as he was told. That is when Shawndra pulled the mask from over her face allowing him to see exactly who she was. The man eyes grew wide from the confirmation of knowing who he was now dealing with. The memory flashed through his head of him beating the shit out of Derek. The man he barely knew. All he knew was that he had fucked his bitch. Well, old bitch and left a seed in her womb to grow. Did he have any regrets in his heart or mind about beating the shit out of Derek? No. Not at all. Well just one. It was that he did not kill both Derek and Shawndra when he had the chance. Now he stared down the barrel of a Smith & Wesson M&P 340 Centennial 357 five shot Magnum Revolver.

"Listen, little shawty, that shit dead with me and dude. I promise." He begins to do the only logical thing there was to do at a moment like this, plead. "You ain't gone much worry about me no more. I put that shit on my life."

"Shut the fuck up," Shawndra spat back. "Ain't nobody trying to hear that shit. You ain't so tough now are you, pussy?" Shawndra spoke through clenched teeth. On the low, see has been craving to quench this thirst for blood that she has had since her last kill which was her first one. It was like an unreachable itch not being able to kill again. She constantly had battles in her mind about the fact of her becoming a monster. One side of herself argued that she did what she had to at that moment. That she would close that chapter of her life and never read those pages again. On the other side, she dreamed of the day she would be able to do it again. She could not wait. She was anticipating it like a pregnant woman in her final stages of pregnancy. The day Derek was randomly attacked, Shawndra knew then that she would hunt this man down like a lioness chasing her prey. Just to rip him apart like a breakup letter in the hands of a broken heart. Now that the time has come, she felt as if she could cum on herself from the excitement. It gave her a rush that she just could not explain. In fact, it confused her. How could something that was supposed to be so wrong make her feel so good? It was the best form of ecstasy she had ever felt in her life up to this point.

"This a be the last chance to get to put anything on your life. I can bet you that. In fact, I can promise it to you. But then again, you cannot bet on something that you do not have. Now, can you?" After she asked her question Shawndra laughed wickedly. So much so that she did not even recognize her own voice. "But you right about one thing." she tightened her grip on the handle of the pistol a little more and held the weapon steadily aiming it at the middle of his forehead. "That shit between you and my man is dead." Bow! A single bullet exploded from the muzzle of the pistol and joined forces with the man's brain as it penetrated his skull. His body tumbled to the asphalt of the parking lot. Shawndra lowered the gun. Now taking aim at his torso, Shawndra placed four more holes into his body as she dumped the remaining bullets out of the gun. "Can't beef when you can't breathe, dummy."

From there Shawndra dashed to a car that she had borrowed from her best friend, Kadesha. With her adrenaline, as well as her feet, she made it to her car. Once there, she hoped in. Wisely, she left the vehicle running which allowed her to immediately throw the gear into the drive and speed out of the apartment complex. When she made it to the main road, she slowed the car down and drove the normal speed limit. At this time of night or morning, however you viewed it, the traffic was so light that it was barely any at all. Shawndra used this this time alone to gather her thoughts back together. Checking all her mirrors, she noticed that she was way in the clear. An evil smile had grown across her face as she played back the murder over and over in her mind. The blood splashing all over her face was something like a cleansing for her. The image of the body lying lifeless on the ground gave a powerful sensation that was hard for her to find anywhere else. She loved it all. But for now, she would have to put those feelings that she loved so much back into the closet. Because as much as she loved her newfound fetish, it was something that no one could find out about. For one, she would hate to have to deal with the harsh consequences that come with the deadly sin that she loves so much. And secondly, she could not imagine what people would think of her if they found out that she was a cold-blooded heartless killer. Although her killings were rightfully justified with sound reason. Still, she knew some people just would not understand.

Once entering the backdoor of Derek's apartment, the first thing Shawndra did was examine the clock hanging from the wall in the kitchen, which currently read three forty-two with the second's hand closely ticking its way to another cycle around the clock. She closed and locked the door behind herself and placed her keys on the kitchen table in a bowl along with Derek's. Next, she quietly tipped toed her way up the stairs. Once she got to the top, she kept straight ahead right into the bathroom. Her clothes were already there waiting for her stationed in a drawer the was built into the toilet storage. She turned the handle to the shower and gave the water the time it needed to get hot. While she waited, she stood in front of the mirror and had begun to pull the clothes off her body. As she slowly uncovered her almost unblemished skin, she came face to face with herself in the mirror. The only marks on her body were the ones left by Tank. A burnt mark on her shoulder. A few healing marks on her neck from his fingernails deeply cutting into her skin as he choked her. And a few more. Silently, she whimpered for her soul. Even after getting away freely fleeting from the scene of her second murder, she somehow still felt like she was in big trouble. The reason being was because she knew that she had a troubling hunger to feed from here on out. She could not think of a way to kick the habit she had. And the scariest thing about it was that she did not even want to. It made her feel strangely more important suddenly. It gave her a powerful feeling that she did not want to hand over. She felt more connected to her inner being like a person who had just realized what their life purpose was. These emotions placed her back at one again like the true meaning to atonement.

The fogging of the mirror and rising of the heat in the small bathroom gave Shawndra confirmation that the water was ready for her body. Before she stepped into the tub, she made sure scooped up the small bottle of bleach that she had already placed beside the toilet. She knew at least one thing and that was that if she was going to do this murder thing, then she would be one of the smartest that had ever done it. She stood with her back towards the water. Loving the way, the heat gave her body a waking rush, she closed her eyes and thought of murder. Then another thought of significant importance weaved through her mind. It was Derek. She knew that even he could not find out about her actions. She thought that even though it was for him he just would not understand. He would not approve. That he would not accept the new addition to her lifestyle. Or would he. But right now, that just was not something that she was ready to figure out. Waters she was not ready to test.

Shawndra rid herself of the overthinking so she could focus on her present activities. After opening the small bottle of bleach, she poured it over her body starting with her neck and shoulder area. Afterward, she soaked her washcloth with the liquid before lathering it with her favorite soap. Then, she scrubbed her body over twice. Finally, rinsing herself off with the hot water mixed in with the little bleach she had remaining.

From there she dried off, put on her clean clothes, and placed her old ones in a trash bag. She hid the bag in the back of a hallway closet that her and Derek barely ever went into. Later, she planned to remove the bag and take the clothes to a safe place to be burned and destroyed. With cat like movements, she crawled and cuddled underneath her man. Knowing that he was safe to walk outside of his door in the morning in pursuit of achieving his goals safely gave Shawndra security. In his sleep, Derek sensed Shawndra's presence and wrapped his arm around her waist hugging her tightly. She backed her body into his, ass first and got comfortable. She closed her eyes with a peaceful smile on her face as if she had not done any harm at all. Knowing that the two of them would have to be up within the next two hours, she sent her tired body into sleep mode.

***

For the last few days, the tier has been in eerie suspense. Most of the loud screams and yells were turned into whispers or silence. Some anticipated something big to go down on the tier. While most only suspected, very few knew exactly who the target was. As for the rest, they are completely clueless. One thing that was for sure, everyone was sure that trouble was on its way. If not already here. The energy itself waved off a dangerous vibration to all except the one person that it was about to happen to. The way he saw it today was just one of the most laid-back days he had ever witnessed on this tier. He did not trip at all. He loved the vibe. Or so at least that is what he thought.

Once E gave Flex the whole run down, Flex from there had begun putting his plot into order. He had niggas on standby just for shit like this. They could never wait too long before they almost went crazy from the lack of what they called recreation. Come to think about it, they were so excited about the news of them being able to make a move that it made them eagerly irritated. But for incredibly wise reasons, the hit would be appointed at a certain day and time.

The delayed Black on Black violence was due to the needed preparation for lockdown. E wanted to get at least another cycle of strips off though out the jail before their tier went on lockdown for God knows how long. Everyone else who had a say so agreed with the wait. They wanted time to make sure they were able to go to the canteen and fill up their bags with lockdown foods. Additionally, those who used the drugs wanted to make sure that they had their orders in on their drugs of choice. Whichever drug it was, most of them all agreed that all drugs went best with a cigarette. Amid the waiting period for the attack, E was able to get rid of two-hundred and fifty Suboxones. Even with lowering the prices down to only one-hundred dollars, he was still able to accumulate twenty-five thousand dollars. Just as soon as the last batch was gone, he was getting another set of strips in. He already had in mind that he would save this set of strips for after lockdown. He knew damn well that the people on the tier would run out of whatever they had brought from him before going in. And how was most certain that the niggas on another tiers would barley be able to wait for his unit to be back off lockdown. His plan was, for when that time came, to hike the prices back up on the strips. Making about thirty-three percent more than what he made on the current run.

"Aye E," Flex called for his cellie's attention. E had just hung up the phone trying to come up with a plan. They were so calculated that Flex already knew what the phone call was about. Once E was by Flex's side at the poker table which was Flex's favorite spot on the tier, Flex asked for E's ear. Of course, he did not want everyone in their business. They both felt as if everyone knew too much as it is. But you could not but a hush on energy. No worries though because as long as no one tipped the target off, it was cool. Everyone knew that if they had done such a thing that they would be figured out. And that once they were figured out, then they would be next to go.

"Everything straight?" Flex asked E. The question was a throw off. One that could have had waited. But Flex wanted to peep who was trying extra hard to listen in.

"Yeah, that shit a go," E replied. "Shawty ass locked in for sure."

"Already. Go check the weather for us. I think the storm coming in around this time."

"Already," E replied already knowing what Flex was getting at. Therefore, his next move from there was to the CO's desk.

"What's up, sexy?" He asked Crawford. She smiled. That was a good enough response for him. "What is the word? You know it is raining in the forecast today, right? A thunderstorm on the way. With all this dirt out around here, shit can get muddy. I'ma need you to stay in the clear."

Crawford understood everything that E had just said. The fact of the matter was that he was not speaking of a literal storm. And she knew exactly what he was saying and asking.

"Yeah, it's all clear on my end." She gave an answer to the question E asking was the hit a go. Basically, waiting on Crawford to give the green light. "And I am Gucci. About to go on lunch break anyway." She answered another. "You make sure you stay safe and out the way."

"Shawty, you know I am going to be good. I'ma miss your sexy ass though." E threw in a meaningful flirtatious compliment attempting to lighten the mood.

"For what? Two days. Three." Crawford functioned as if she was unimpressed. The actual truth was different though.

"Hell yeah!" E blurted out along with a light laugh. "That is a long time for me not to be seeing you. Shit, that is why I be walking around this bitch mad as a motherfucker on your days off."

"Yeah, I bet." Crawford expressed with a heavy blush. "Got a bitch up in here on her days off and shit like that, begging to get drafted and some more. I'm snatching up all types of overtime." At the end of her comment, Crawford had joined in with E's laughter.

"Shidd... I hope that ain't no complaint. Especially with the way you bring that bag in. I do not think you should be complaining at all."

"Naw. No complaints, boo. None. Matter fact—"

"Thank you, E." He had cut her words off in the middle of her sentence. Only to replace them with the same words she was about to use anyway. "I know I know," he said with the least bit of arrogance. "Alright, little mama," He slapped his hand on top of the wooden horseshoe shaped desk. "It's about time for daddy to go and play karma." Immediately after his last word, E was walking off heading back in Flex's direction. During his travels, E caught eye contact with Flex. He simply gave an exceptionally light head nod. Flex knew from there that the light was green for the jail house hit to go into motion. Flex nodded back so subtly that it was almost unnoticeable. He then waved over one of his youngins on the tier. His age was almost minor compared to the other men on the tier. But his body size was bigger than at least half of the tier. He bopped on his way to answer the call from Flex. Once he reached his destination, Flex whispered something in his ear. The youngin grew excited and then found his way to his partner in crime like, they were codefendants to each other's case. The youngin then passed the word to his partner. They both grew excited at the breaking news. All they have been doing is bragging on who was going to fuck the man up the worst. Everyday, all day that is how their conversation went for the many long hours they were awake. It has been days of them patiently waiting to do serious harm to somebody or anybody. Especially, someone who deserved it.

The sound of the tier doors sliding open alerted the whole tier. They all had stopped what they were doing just to look up at the door. Crawford had her key in the keyhole allowing the door's mechanics to do its job. The youngins got even more hyped up. They knew it was time to play. To them it seemed as if it took the doors forever to open. They could not wait for Crawford to exit the tier. Crawford took her time, allowing the door to slide all the way open before she walked through them. Even once she had passed the door seal, she still had to close the door back the same way she had opened it. Along with proceeding the very same procedure with the second door of the tier. As the doors were closing, Crawford stared at E through the double glass windows. She hoped that he would be okay. And that he would be smart enough to take her advice and stay out of the way. She would hate for him to jeopardize everything they had built up until this point. With her knowing that this was only the beginning, she also knew that it was plenty more money to make down the line. She was not too big on taking a risk to lose what she was risking doing. Just did not make any sense to her at all. But if her judgement of character was correct, E was smart and focused. Just like she needed him to be.

As soon as Crawford had started to make her way down the hallway, the youngins were making their way towards their victim. The whole tier kept their eyes on the two of them. Some people were even hoping and praying that they were not the suspect's target, saying another prayer once they walked straight past them. The seconds ticked by very slowly from the suspicion. Wisely, a few people had moved away from the target. While others were heading over to their cell doors, making sure to stay clearly out of the way.

The first of the two youngins drew the first blow. By cocking back, a powerful punch and hammering the victim square in his face. It caught the man completely off guard. He never even thought about being attacked for one minute. For one, he was just as sure as a federal conviction that his horrible past was covered up deeply enough for no one to be able to dig up. But he could not have been further away from the truth even if it were on the other side of the earth.

The victim stumbled backwards a bit and grabbed his eye. His vision went blank and then it came back to within a matter of a second. He looked up to set his eyes on his attacker. Before he could even defend himself, he was catching another blow. This time it came from the other side, causing his temple to throb immediately. He covered up the side of his face hoping to block the upcoming blow. Instead, he was hit square in the chin by an upper cut that rattled his brain. You could already notice the rattle on his face from the few hits. He grew fatigued quicker than an asthmatic on a sprint. Too bad for him, he was not even halfway through the battle. The punches start to come faster as well as harder. He could have sworn that someone else, if not two more people had lent helping hands in his ass whooping. He made a wish for it to stop but it only grew worse.

A heavy fist to the victim's wide open nose caused him to lean backwards a bit. It was just enough for him to catch a blustering four knuckles to his now exposed chest. Equitably as his chest was wide, it was now caved in from the powerful blow. He gasped deeply trying to catch his breath. He placed an open palm hand on his chest simultaneously catching a sharp hook to his gut. He doubled over and finally tumbled to the floor. Their fist was replaced with feet as the two youngins went immediately to stomping the man out on the floor. The sufferer did the wisest thing he could do now, which was to ball up like a little bitch in the middle of the floor and take the kicks as best as he could. His body was in major pain. He realized that his arm was wet due to blood leaking from his mouth and nose. The man begun to settle in the moment, enduring as much of the pain as he could. He thought that if this was the worst of it, then he would be able to live through it. Besides, help should be on the way soon anyway.

As if he was cursed, every time he thought that things could not have gotten any worse, it did. Suddenly, the man felt a sharp poke in the side of his rib. A third man had come along with a banger and penetrated the defenseless man in his side. The victim let out a howling cry for help. But of course, no one did. Instead, another stab, and another, and another. Now, the man cried for sure. Tears twinkled down his face like a drizzle on a windshield. If he never had any regret before, he sure was begging the Lord for forgiveness now.

Finally, a prayer answered.

"Everybody get to their fucking cells!" A white shirt lieutenant commanded as she came through the door with a gang of COs behind her. They were armed with guns containing rubber bullets inside of it ready to shoot, along with tear gas and pepper spray. "Now! All y'all!"

Once the small group of people had pulled out of the crowd, it was easier for the jail's staff to see the body balled up on the ground in a pool full of blood. The vision pissed the LT off even more than she already was. Her inmates were moving, but fast enough for her liking. "I swear to Jesus, if I have to say it one more time, these rubber bullets gone fire faster than a match drop into a pile of gasoline. Now, move!" The men moved along a little faster with the threat. But they could not leave without saying their goodbyes to their least favorite detainee.

"Pussy bitch!"

"Get the fuck out of here, fucking chomo!"

"Bet you won't do that again."

"Don't bring your ass back down here neither, boy"

"You like little kids, don't you?"

"You smoke crack, don't you?" Another man questioned, mocking the principal from the movie Lean on Me. The men got a good laugh out of that one.

"He sleep!"

"Naw, that nigga dead."

"I hope his ass is dead. Fucking fuck boy."

"Aye youngins, y'all little niggas did that!" An old head had shouted out to the youngins who had put the work in, not just for the whole tier, but the world.

"No bullshit!" Another man had yelled out in agreement. The rest gave a round of applause as a handful of COs dragged the young bucks off the tier.

"Free the gang!" A member of the youngsters' peer group shouted.

"Alright, alright. Enough of that shit. Show's over now," a Sergeant spoke as he was placing the inmates into their cells. To be honest, he was pleased with the deed that had just been done. He was not alone but they all had a job to do.

"Get somebody down here to clean up this mess." The Sergeant urged now that the wounded man was carried out of the pod.

E and Flex dapped up with their backs against the wall in the back of the tier where their cell door was. From a distance Crawford eyed E and he gave her the look back. "Y'all two in the back!" Crawford yelled out. "What y'all think y'all special? In the cell, now!" She yelled through the tier. The two looked at each other and laughed aloud but did exactly what they were told. Power was a wonderful feeling.

***

"Oh my God. I was only one pin away from a strike. That was the closest I came to getting it. I cannot, I am too damn drunk y'all." Destiny was smiling and having the time of her life. Accompanying her was her cousin, Josephine, also known as Jo, her cousin's boyfriend, Carter, and Shy. Currently they were taking up a lane of bowling at The Park RVA. The place was becoming the spot to be for the weekend's nightlife in Richmond. Before bowling, the couples had indulged in a few games of putt-putt, took a swing at virtual golf, and even expressed their talents in karaoke. Not to mention, devouring delectable meals like garlic and parm wings, chicken, and waffles sandwiches. Plus, some of the best desserts they had ever had in their lives. Enjoying it all while sipping signature cocktails, wines, and different tequilas. To sum it all up, the night was lit.

"Okay, it' your turn now, Shy!" Destiny spoke with plenty of laughter. He could tell that she was happy with enjoying the moment. "While you over there just chilling like you all cool and stuff."

Shy was practically laid back on the couch gazing at Destiny's every move. He loved the way she lit up every time she smiled. The way she smiled every time she felt happiness. Her happiness was expressed freely without feeling the need to hold it back. He sensed not one sign of misery in her soul. It was pure. He realized it was a feeling he urged for without even understanding why. He loved the comfortableness he felt from being around her, yet it placed him in the state of unease. These paradox emotions left Shy in a state of irrational confusing. What was even more unexplainable was that he was in no rush at all to figure out why.

"Uhh," Shy asked no one in particular. Snapping back into his body. "Yeah, y'all should already know what I'm on by now." He stood up and walked over to the ball rack and to choose his new favorite bowling ball. "Y'all paying attention, right?" Shy asked, making his way now to the lane. Next, he took aim and tossed the heavy ball. It started to roll as soon as it hit the floor. Shy took a few steps back as smoothly as he could while keeping his eye on the ball, not really trying too hard. That is just how his demeanor was. Once he felt satisfied with the looks of things, he turned around, "Yeah, that's it," he said confidently. Not a hint of arrogance in his words at all.

The ball collided into the pins.

"Okay, another strike!" Carter exclaimed as if it was him receiving the points for the turn. He let out a laugh that ended up being contagious to the rest of them.

"I'm already knowing," Shy stated right before taking a seat next to Destiny on the couch. "I can teach you the game if you want me too," he offered her his help. They made eye contact that sent a rush of emotions through both of their bodies.

"Yeah, I'ma need some help with this one." Destiny accepted. "And you better show me right." She giggled. "Do not leave out a single detail. I need all the tips. Then I'ma beat you with your own game."

"Oh yeah?" Shy simply asked behind his laughter. "I ain't even tripping though," he said honestly. "If you win, I win."

"And how you figure that?"

"Cause if winning keeps you happy, then I'm winning."

"Awwww. Oh, so you trying to win win?"

"I can't do it, if I don't do it right."

"I know that's right." Destiny agreed.

"Alright, Destiny. It is your turn." Jo-Jo called out to her favorite cousin.

"You ready?" Shy asked on his way to getting up off the couch. Destiny nodded her head shyly as if she were a little embarrassed. Shy held out his hand.

"Come on. Let us make it happen then." Destiny grabbed his hand and Shy pulled her up off the couch.

"First you wanna grab the ball that make you feel the most comfortable."

Destiny picked up the medium size ball and looked at Shy. "That's the one?" He made sure before they proceeded. She nodded once more to confirm her answer. Afterwards, led her to the lane.

"Now it is important to have your vision locked in. If you can see it happen before it does, then you have completed half of the challenge. Set your focus on exactly what you want to happen and lock your aim on your target." Shy gave Destiny a few seconds for her mental preparation. "You ready now?" Shy questioned just for assurance. Destiny nodded again like a little girl being asked if she wanted to take a trip to the carnival. "Alright, let's go." Shy stood behind her and wrapped his hands around her. Using both of his hands, he gripped the lower parts of her arms. "You want to stand up straight, make sure your posture is good. Now as you lift the ball up, bring it eye level, and it is best if you put just a little hump into your back." He leans Destiny's body slightly over helping her bend to the perfect angle. "Make sure that you're able to see the pins in the background of the ball." Shy was a natural at most things and bowling just added to his lengthy list of talents. So, explaining the techniques was second nature to him. While explaining though, he noticed that his natural nature was waking uncontrollably. It was almost impossible for any normal man not to become aroused by Destiny natural beauty.

With his pelvis pressed against her backside, it was also almost impossible for Destiny not to feel the manhood poking her in the rearend. "Okay, the real trick is this," the two of them tried to ignore what was obviously happening below the belts. Although, it was heavy on both of their minds. "As you cock the ball back you must remember that this is where all your power comes from. Depending on the amount of power you force behind the ball, determines the speed. A lot of people get it fucked up and think that is what it is all about. Power and speed. But it is not. It is important that you keep your vision, focus, and aim locked." While Shy assisted Destiny in putting the proper moves into motion, he started to move out of her way. "Do not worry about the power. Get your accuracy down first, and the power would come naturally.

Destiny followed through on the instructions that Shy had given her. She released the ball as steadily as she could to strike her target. The ball made a thudding sound as it bounced once off the ground. From there the roll commenced. It was a slow-motion roll. But surprisingly to Destiny it traveled in a straight line. The pair of pairs watched the ball eagerly as it rolled down the lane. It seemed as if the bowling ball took forever to reach the pin as if time had slowed down drastically. It was not a boring wait though. An anxious one instead. Once the ball finally contacted the first ball, it set off a chain reaction. One pin colliding with the next in a frenzy of tumbles. When it was all said and done, not one pin was left standing. Immediately, Destiny expressed a burst of excitement.

"Oh my God! I did that shit, bitch!" She threw her arms up and moved towards Shy. "Thank you so much!" She wrapped her arms around his neck and hugged him tight. He was not shy at all to hug back wrapping his own arms around her waistline and pulling her in a little tighter. "You are a great teacher!"

"That was all you." Shy boosted her confidence. Destiny pulled back and looked into Shy's eyes. "One of the best and hardest things to be is a great learner. You understood the assignment and got it done. All I did was give you the game. You were the one that put it into play."

"I know but…" Destiny started to respond but had just stopped in the middle of her sentence. She gazed into Shy's eyes a little deeper. The feeling was as if she had connected with his soul. "You are really something special, huh." The phrase could have been mistaken for a question. But really Destiny was confirming instead of searching for confirmation. "I've never ever met no one quite like you."

Shy was pleased with the comment, especially coming from her. Truth is though, he had heard the substantial number of times in his young life. Still though, he never grew tired of hearing it. "Dead ass, you will not find another nowhere near me. I come one in a million."

"Yeah, I bet." Destiny refused to protest as she agreed with Shy's comment. As the night proceeded, the couples continued to enjoy what was left of the night that was filled with plenty of laughter and love. Something Shy was not so used to. The more time he spent around Destiny and her family, the more he let his guards down, becoming wrapped up in a drama free lifestyle.

"That was so much fun, thank y'all for coming out with us. Especially you, Shy. I have not seen Destiny that happy since she got accepted into Howard," Jo-Jo explained as the four of them along with a crowd full of other people were spilling out of the doors of The Park RVA.

"You mean the Howard University?" Shy questioned curiously. Destiny was right by his side wrapped underneath his arm. She snuggled against his warm body as they walked along.

"Yeah, I am," Jo-Jo replied. "She's always being so modest as if she doesn't want anybody to know that she goes there—"

"No. It's not that," Destiny cut off Jo-Jo before she was able to finish her sentence. "It is just that people treat you so differently once they find out that I go to that school, especially people like—"

"Well, look," Shy now was the person who was cutting Destiny's speech off midway. "You do not have to worry about that with me. I already told you anyway, that you will not find someone like me. So, whatever you have had to go through with other people you can—"

Boom! Boom! Boom! Three shots rang out into the air causing everyone to freeze for literary a quick half of a second. The first set of shots were followed by another that set off a chain reaction of gun firing. The parking lot went crazy with people running in every direction. Immediately, Shy's survival instinct kicked in. The thing he did first was whip out the gun that he carried in his bag the whole night. Secondly, he gathered his people and instructed them to follow him to his car. Shots had begun to fly too close to Shy's head for his liking. While covering Destiny up for her protection, Shy flung a couple of shots in the direction where most of the bullets had traveled from. Destiny screamed. It quickly went from one of the happiest days in her life to one of the scariest. Shy was not too surprised at how the night was ending. What surprised him is that it was going so great. Although these types of things usually did not happen at the location they were at, you could never be too sure with Richmond.

Shy led his party to the car. Right before they approached, he pushed the button on his key to unlock the doors. "Y'all get in! Hurry up, hurry up!" he themanded. As they filled the car, Shy stood guard right outside of the car. Once everyone was inside, he hopped in a pulled off. There was a scrambling crowd at the edge of the parking lot preventing Shy's car from exiting. He stuck the gun outside the window and aimed it at the clouds. Without thinking twice, he let off a couple of shots into the air. Immediately the crowd got out of the way trying to keep themselves from getting harmed. From there, Shy swerved out of the parking lot and sped away from the chaos.

When he was finally in the clear, Shy reduced the car to the normal speed limit.

"What was that, Shy?" Destiny desperately wanted to know. "And what about our cars!?"

"First of all, I know you scared but you really need to lower your toned when you talking to me." Shy themanded his respect. "We gone come back later when it is safe and get y'all cars. The first thing I thought about was our safety."

"How are you talking about our safety when you are one of the ones carrying the gun? Then you just start shooting out of nowhere like the rest of those gangsters that was out there. Look, I am telling you right now, I am not into all this killing and shit. If you have people after you that are trying to kill you and stuff like that, then you need to keep my people and I as far away from you as possible." Destiny's voice was beginning to crack as she shivered with the aftermath of fear.

Shy reached over with his right hand and placed it on her thigh. Caressing it as it reassured her with his confident words. "I ain't that type of nigga alright. I have a gun because everyone out this bitch have one. Does it make it right? No. But if you were out here daily like I am then it would make plenty of sense to you as well. Ion have people after me trying to kill me or none of that. Am I in that lifestyle? No. But I am connected and around it by force. I must be always ready out here. You never know when a motherfucker gone step on you out here for no apparent reason. So, am I out here looking to do anything to anybody out here? No. But am I prepared and protected? You damn right! Sometimes it is either that or die out this bitch. And that is not an option I am willing to choose."

Destiny was speechless after Shy's short life experience speech. She had only heard of this type of lifestyle but never had front row seats to the action. She was smart enough though to know that what he said did make a lot of sense. What she could not understand though was why one would rather sink into this life. Instead of fighting to live, why not fight to make it out of the circumstances. In her mind, there definitely was a choice. As if she was not in a whirlpool of emotions from the start. Now her emotional blend was like

CRIME PAYS 2 | SELF MADE TAY

cake ingredients being stirred by a mixer. Soon her fear turned into excitement. She was confused as to how. But all the excitement of the roller coaster was heating her up. She felt herself falling even deeper for Shy. The way he themanded his respect. The way he understood and played his position. The way he went straight into superhero mode to save and protect not only her, but her family as well. For a woman who already had her whole life mapped and planned out, who knew exactly what she wanted, one where a man was nowhere in sight of her plans for an exceptionally long time, felt as if she had falling in love. The only thing that scared her was that she was not sure if it was good or bad.

Lesson 2.8
Keep Your Game Tight

Accompanied by Shawndra, Derek pulled up to a house in the Church Hill area of the city. He had an appointment today looking to invest in his first house to get his real estate business going. The money he would use came from Shawndra who had kept the money that Tank had left behind after being murdered. I know one would ask, why would Derek buy a house for business purposes when he does not even have a house to live in. Right, I agree. But Derek had other plans which he saw from the end first. He thought it would be best to get his business off the ground first so he would be able to buy Shawndra and himself the house of their dreams. Instead of buying a house and struggling to take care of it. That just did not make any sense to him. So, here he was stepping out in the most affordable three-piece suit that his current money could buy with Shawndra on his arm to compliment the deal. She wore a stunning dress that you may have thought cost a lot of money. But it was her own body that made the dress look better and more expensive instead of it being the other way around.

"Mr. Brown, good morning. How are you doing?" A white man in a pair of dress pants with a white shirt and tie walked outside of the front door of the house. He flicked his arm up and looked at the plain jane red faced Rolex. "Two minutes earlier, that's a great start." The man stood on the porch awaiting Derek's approach so he can guide him around the house. "And who is this beautiful lady of love I'm being graced with the opportunity to lay my eyes upon?" He asked admiring Shawndra's appeal.

"Tim Warner," Derek returned the greeting. "Good morning to you as well. And please, never mind the two minutes." He waved off, "This is on time for me." Once the two men were face to face, they shook hands with tight grips looking each other in the eyes as a show of respect. "And this beautiful blessing by my side is my lady of course."

Shawndra held her hand out for Tim Warner to shake. Once he gripped her hand, he raised it up. Instead of shaking it, he placed a kiss on the back of her hand before lowering it back to Shawndra's side. He took a long couple seconds to analysis it.

"Well, I do not see a ring here. I advise you hurry and make that move before someone else tries to claim your prize." The three of them shared laughs at the light joke.

"Thank you for that," Shawndra showed an act of gratitude. "But trust me, he does not have anything to worry about. The way he loves me is more than enough for now. And trust me, I am not worried at all myself. I have plenty faith that when he is ready that he will make the smart decision."

"Hmm, beauty and brains," Tim said more to himself than to Derek. "Yeah, she needs a ring immediately." They laughed some more.

"Well, Mr. Warner after this deal falls through, I'll be more than able to do just that," Derek replied.

"Speaking of that," Mr. Warner said as if he had forgotten the reason for the gathering in the first place, "If you are ready, we can get to the business." From there he led the two through the door of the house. "As we already discussed, this house will need a lot of work done to it." The first room was the den. It was accessible as soon as you walked through the front door of the house. "It has a lot a potential to be a stately home. Built in fireplace which I am sure you can use for a great accessory. Once you fix it up nicely right, you will already have your buyers sold. Also, there is a half bathroom right here. Perfect place to have meetings or conversations. The guest will not have to go any further than this room if the homeowner does not want them to. You can take care of so many things just from this room here."

The next room was the living room which was twice the size of the den. Mr. Warner showed the best parts of the room as well as what needed to be done to it. The kitchen was next before they headed out to the backyard. The tour was finally complete once they all came from upstairs and checked out the two rooms and full bathroom.

"So, Mr. Brown, if you like what you see, we can talk more about closing the deal. Get the paperwork done and the house will be all yours." They were sitting on the porch of the house when a twill Carbon Fiber black and grey Urus Lamborghini pulled up right in front of the house. It was so exclusive that it caught the attention of all their eyes.

"Ohh," Mr. Warner said as if he was surprised. "Didn't think that he would show up," he said indicating that he obviously knew exactly who the person was. "He is always late. But after being this late I thought he would not show at all." The operator of the expensive vehicle stepped out in a stunting Stefano Ricci evening jacket with a pair of slacks to match.

"Jeffery, hey! How are you doing friend!"

"Warner, how are you doing on this splendid, lovely day? You ready to get this deal done?" Jeffery was stepping on the curb to the sidewalk making his way to the porch. As he did so, he tugged on his expensive jacket as an act of straightening it up, as if it could get any straighter. It was perfectly fitted as if it was tailor made. "There is no need for a walk through and all that other professional stuff you always like to get into. You already know I want it. So, just name the price so we can get this done."

Jeffery was a real estate investor. And may I add, a phenomenally successful one at that. Not only that though because that was just one of his smaller businesses. He had a few. To say the least, the man was swimming in money like a Scrooge McDuck. He was just as greedy as the Disney character as well. Now he stood on the porch face to face with Mr. Warner. He ignored Derek and Shawndra as if they were not even there to be visible in the first place. Pen in the right hand, Jeffery held his checkbook in the other prepared to place the numbers on the slip of paper.

The act puzzled both Shawndra and Derek. First, they were unaware that people even still wrote checks these days and time. Another thing that bothered the two was how this unknown man had the audacity to stand with his back to them as if they were not even there.

Shawndra paid remarkably close attention to everything about the man. From his demeanor , his appearance, the way he used his words, and the car he drove. The license plate number. TPA-67JP, she repeated over and over in her mind. She did not really have an intention to use the numbers, but she wanted to remember them just in case. Her women's intuition was telling her that this lovely business meeting was about to turn sharply left.

"Well, Mr. Mann," Mr. Warner said, talking to Jeffery. "I already have a potential buyer here and we were just about to close up the deal as you pulled up," Mr. Warner spoke up honestly.

Jeffery turned around quickly as if this was really his first time noticing they had company. "Oh, how are you two doing? Nice day we're having huh?" As if he wasn't the one imposing in on their business meeting. After saying those few words, he turned back around just as fast as he looked back. "Looks like we just might have a bidding war. You know how much I love those. Okay, so what are they offering?" he asked, throwing the question towards Mr. Warner.

"Thirty-thousand dollars," Mr. Warner answered. Derek only had fifty thousand to spend. The was the totality of money Derek had from Shawndra when Tank was murdered. He chose this house purposely because it is run down and broken. That made the house extra cheap. His plan was to put the other twenty thousand dollars into renovating the house. Upping the value of the house to at least seventy thousand dollars, making a nice profit so that he would be able to do it all over again.

"Oh, that's it?" Jeffery Mann questioned as if that was nothing. It sort of was not compared to the money he had. He scribbled a combination of letters and words on the slip of paper that was better known as a check. Without even asking what he wanted, or if it was even okay for him to make an offer, he ripped the check out of its book and handed it over to Mr. Warner. "Here you go. Thirty-five thousand. It is a little extra for you."

Mr. Warner was tempted to take the check, but he hesitated. Before he was even able to say a word.

"I'll give you forty!" Derek blurted out, making the window on his spending and profit margin just that slimmer. Shawndra nudged Derek in his side trying to get him to remain quiet and allow Jeffery to close the deal. But it was too late.

"Ohh, that's what I'm talking about." Jeffery grew excited. After balling up the first check in his hand, he threw it off to the side landing it in the small yard of grass. He used the next blank check and wrote another one. "Forty-five thousand," Jeffery said, handing the second check over the Mr. Warner. At the time he did not even think about taking the paper. He had been in enough of these situations to know where this could go. And no matter who would be the one to win the bidding, it would only mean a win for him. A big one at that. The only thing was that Derek had not spoken again. He had finally got the whiff of what Shawndra was trying to get him to realize.

Derek's silence forced Mr. Warner to take the check. "Well, Mr. Mann congratulations on closing the deal. If you want, we can take a seat and get the paperwork done or—"

"Come on Warner," Jeffery sliced the businessman's sentence in half enabling him to talk any further. "You know how I do business. This is not our first rodeo." With that, Jeffery headed down the few flights of stairs. "Better luck next time rookies," he said to Derek and his woman, rubbing the win in their faces. "That was easier than I thought." He hopped into his car and pulled off feeling highly accomplished. As he rolled away, Shawndra eyed his license plate one final time, making a photogenic memory of the plate, writing it down in her mind. TPA-67JP.

"I am so sorry about that, Mr. Brown. I would hope that you can under—"

"No." Derek was now the next man to cut off Mr. Warner's word. "There is really no need to explain. It is business, right? I totally understand. I will just continue to check the market and find something else. Although it was a challenge to come across this type of house, with the money that I have to offer, I am up for it. If you have something that you think I may be interested in, please contact me, and let me know. Come on bae, let us go." Derek grabbed Shawndra's hand and led her back to their vehicle.

***

Lil' One stood under a tree on the corner of Mosby and R street. That was the same block where BM had murdered Lil' One's best friend and tried on his own life. The person he was searching for was BM of course. He had already been out there for about an hour at least walking up and down the street in hopes that he would see the person he hated the most in this world. The only thoughts in his mind was what would happen once he finally caught up with BM. He envisioned dumping the whole clip into his skull, shattering it like broken glass. But he was growing tired of waiting, walking, and standing around. It was starting to feel as if he was chasing a ghost. He knew that this was the spot where BM was trapping. He moved around after the shooting he finally considered, just maybe. Also, he remembered the word on the street that BM was on a mission of taking over the whole Mosby. So, there was no telling where this nigga could be. On top of that, once he did finally lay eyes on his target, Lil' One was smart enough to know that he would not be alone.

All these different thoughts were flowing through the young mind of Lil' One as he kept his eyes on the streets and the people that traveled through them. When he made his way over here from Hill Side, none of these things he was now thinking of was a factor to him at all. For some reason, he was beginning to wise up. This made him angry because he realized that this may not be as easy as he thought it would be. Then, something happened that gave him hope. He saw something, or someone, that could hand him an opportunity to change his whole approach. A way to switch up his attack from super aggressive and turn it into a back door action. The two young ladies that he locked his vision on were coming from down the street. It was just the same as he had remembered when he first laid eyes on the two of them. It was Lil' One who spotted them first as he and Crow were chilling in the rental car that Keem had provided for them. Crow warned Lil' One to leave the two young ladies alone, but he did not listen as he never did. Now, thinking back on the day, Lil' One could almost swear that those two were the reason his best friend was dead. If not the reason, then they played a major part in the distraction. Lil' One could have murdered them both right now if he were not getting back into his right mind. But it just would not make any sense. Instead, though, he would give the two a chance to pay him back for that evil sin he committed against his friend and self.

"What's up with y'all two?" He said from under the tree. He had one leg kicked up on the base of the tree.

The two young women had already spotted Lil' One from a distance without knowing exactly who he was. The thing that caught their eyes was his drip. The next thing was the smell of the loud gas that floated through the air. "Girl, that shit gas," Bianca had said a little before they were too close to Lil' One. "Who you talking too?" She asked a stupid question as if they were not the only three people standing out there in the cool air. Lil' One had a fitted cap over his braids. The brim of the hat had shadowed half of his face, making his identity hard to notice. Especially, to someone who had only seen him once.

"I'm talking too your little sexy ass," he stated with an obvious flirt that made Bianca blush a little.

"Uhh, girl he is at your ass," Kiora said just excited as her friend was feeling.

"Shidd, I'm dead ass at both of y'all ass to keep it a hundred." Lil' One was being honest. The only thing was that he was not at them the way they may have thought he meant it.

"Ohh, naw girl this nigga got big balls," Bianca replied.

"You ain't seen shit yet." Lil' One promised.

"What you think this is a—"

"How about this, let us talk about this over a blunt of loud. I think that would help y'all think clearer. You feel me?"

"You think you can get us by just throwing a blunt of weed in our faces?"

"Naw that ain't about nothing. I come with way more than that. I have a lot to offer. The real question is, what can y'all do for me?"

"I'on know," Bianca spoke up for the both. Without even noticing, they were already agreeing to the fact of Lil' One having them both as his inamoratas. "Let me talk to my best friend right quick. Hold up, wait right here."

"Go ahead. I ain't going nowhere. Trust me." Lil' One promised. He knew that just the fact they were walking off to have a private conversation with each other, that he had. If it were not that, they would have easily shut him down from the jump.

"Girl, this nigga is fine," Bianca said eagerly. "And it looks like he got some money."

"Yeah, I can see that," Kiora replied. "But girl his ass tripping if he thinks his ass is going to have both of us. This ain't that type of party." Bianca laughed.

"Girl his ass ain't getting both of us. His ass will be lucky if he gets one of us. I am saying let us fuck with him and see where this shit goes. Have a little fun with his little ass. And shit, why not give him both of us if it is worth it? It could be fun. The nigga ain't our man. We do not even know this nigga."

"That is the thing bitch, we do not know him from Adam or Eve. And speaking of knowing him, this nigga does not look familiar?"

Bianca took a quick look back. "No," she denied. "I'on think I ever seen his ass before. Why, you think you know him or something?"

"No. But that is the crazy thing. I feel like I do."

Lil' One stood in the same spot he was in for the past twenty minutes or so. He now spent about two of them minutes waiting for the two of the girls to produce a decision that he knew they already had the answer to. He took puff after puff until he noticed them making their way back to him.

"Come on. Follow us!" Bianca simply ordered. Without any protest or procrastination, he did just that. From there, he began to formulate a real plan in his head. One that had the potential to be a lot more solid. If nothing, he knew for sure that he would get an ass load of information out of these two. Just with them talking to each other alone. It is on. Was the main thought he held in his mind. All he had to do was play his cards right, be patient, and do not fuck this up. Who knew where things could go from here?

Lesson 2.9
Loyalty Takes You Far

"But see Mia, that's why I fuck with you the long way." Keem was riding shotgun in his own Rover as he allowed Mia to control the wheel. They were riding through the city doing pickups. He did that with Mia from time to time, one of the most trusted soldiers on his team. The reason being was the fact that he wanted to pop up on his workers every now and then to show face. "You always been about the business. And I hope I am not jinxing your loyalty when I say this, but I felt as if I could always trust you."

Mia laughed a little as she made a left turn at the light. "Jinx my loyalty?" That was a question. But it was more like a statement. "My loyalty is under my total control. And when it comes to you Keem, I cannot name too many that have been here for me like you have. I mean, there is my mother of course. But, outside of that my nigga… Ion even thinks I need to speak on what it is with us. That is why I would rather just show you. Day in and day out I am out here in these streets making sure I do what I must do to make sure the team prosper."

The two had just made their last pick up. They were now pulling up to their trap house headquarters on Lynhaven Avenue. "Nigga! You made sure I had a house to live in. Not an apartment, but a house, my nigga. You made sure my car got paid off. And fuck all the materialistic shit, you also made sure we got that get back on the nigga that took my brother out."

"You know you do not ever have to speak on none of that shit. Especially that last situation. All that shit you got was because of you. Shit that you deserve. Bottom-line though, as long as you continue to work hard and remain loyal, the sky is the limit for you. For us. But come on though. Get that out the trunk and take it in the spot. And hurry up for me so we can make sure we on time to see this fool."

As Mia did as she was told, Keem went through his phone while waiting on her return. It ain't take long. She never made him wait long. She hopped back into the car and placed the car in the driving gear. "Alright, let's go." Within the next thirty minutes or so, the pair were pulling up to their destination. "You want me to take your car to the crib? Or put it in the storage?"

"Shidd, for real you can hold it down for me if you want to," Keem answered. "Pop the trunk for me so I can get my bag. And make sure you keep an eye on all of them niggas' count too."

"You already know I got you, boss. Say no more. And enjoy the next couple of days."

"Ain't nothing to enjoy besides the opportunity. Love fam. Hit my jack if you need me." Before Keem stepped out of the car, he did their secret handshake with Mia that ended it with a salute.

"Love fam. Say no more," Mia replied.

Keem got out of one car and climbed into another. Awaiting him in the back seat of that car was Mac. He was dressed as usual which would be considered unusual to the usual.

"Keem," Mac spoke as soon as the door closed to the car. "I appreciate your early timing. We have a long ride ahead of us. In time, we will be able to get a great amount of conversation out of the way. Both business and personal. The car drove off and they were on their way. As Mac had said, along the way Keem and Mac spoke about a bunch of things. Catching up on what seemed late to both and even making some plans. Exactly two hours and eighteen minutes later, the vehicle was pulling up to its destination. It was a house in the hills of Leesburg, Virginia. The house was mostly made of glass. While the rest was covered in fancy expensive wood. "Come on, step out. Let us look at the lovely house. "A six-million-dollar house on two thousand acres." Mac and Keem stood right outside the car facing the large house. "Ironically, this house was owned by an ex-drug lord back in the eighties. Would you believe that?"

"Yeah, that's crazy," Keem replied simply.

"Now, it is mine. I own it. See, you must have a backup plan for when you are ready to get out of this life that we live. Because, if you think that this shit is a lifetime lifestyle then you will be shit out of luck. We must use this as a steppingstone to get up out of the life we live or was raised from."

Keem stood there taking in all the game they way he always did whenever Mac taught him. To the average mind, one would assume that Mac was doing this for stunting purposes only. But Keem was wise enough to know the true motives behind his action. He trusted that Mac's intentions were pure motivational.

"Come on, let me show you the inside." From there, they walked up to the house and entered the large double doors.

Lesson 2.10
Formulate A Plan

It has been weeks now since the snitch was removed from the tier. The tier was only on lock down for a couple of days. Since then, the vibes on the tier have been so much at ease, that a lot of the men almost would forget that they were incarcerated. On the business side of things, it has been better than ever. Following through with his plan, E had raised the price on the next two or three loads that had come through. Then, lowered them back down to a more reasonable price. That part of the plan was only temporary as well before he had planned to push the price back to his regular margin.

Other than that, everything was everything. E and Flex were becoming closer by the day, especially since the incident had taken place. So much so, that E had a chance to obtain his own cell but refused and opted to stay in with Flex instead. They came to realize that they were an effective team together.

Another bond that E was becoming closer with by the day as well was Tiara Crawford. The business plans the two of them had put together were flawless. Once the one flaw they did have was removed, everything else worked itself out smoothly. That being so, it allowed them more time to discuss and focus on the feelings that they were catching for one another. Occasionally, E would have to catch himself and slow down the flow of his own emotions. He did not want to get so caught up in his emotions that he lost focus on the mission.

***

"What we gone do about some more work?" The young nigga Bank had asked BM. Most of YNT were gathered in the kitchen of their main trap house. "I am down to my last couple of grams. That is why I came in for a few. I know this shit gone go fast as a bitch."

"No bullshit," Tru agreed. "We got shit moving faster than a cheater chasing its prey. You ever make that move you told us that you were gone get done?"

"Who the fuck y'all niggas think y'all are? Asking me questions and shit like that. I got this shit," BM snapped. It was for two reasons though. One was because his members really had the nerve to question him like he had just stated. "Ain't I'm the motherfucker that put you fucking rag dogs on y'all fucking feet?" He asked without really looking for an answer. "I know what the fuck I'm doing." He half lied. The truth was only half because true indeed he did have a plan, but only halfway knew how to follow through to it. One plan was short term. Something that would allow his team time enough before it was time for him to execute his long-term plan. As well as giving it time for the plan all come together. "We about to put this shit together right now as a matter of fact," BM said. "It's time."

"That's what the fuck I'm talking about," Bank said excitedly as he rubbed his itching palms together. There was nothing he loved more in the world than a chance to make some money. "So, what you need us to do, boss man?"

"Get back to the basics," BM simply replied. "I need y'all asses to get back out there on the block and dump the rest of them packs. We need all the money we can put together for this next run. Trust me."

"But I thought we already had the money for the next re-up and we were just waiting on you to make the move?" That Tru being curious as he truly was.

"See, that is exactly why I am the motherfucking boss. Because I think a few steps ahead of you niggas," BM replied with a little animosity but with no force at all. Instead, his words were one of a genius scientist who had a strategy that no one would think of working. "Matter fact, when y'all get out there on the block tell Shoota I said to pull up on me. I am about to take a trip and need him with me."

The two youngins did as they were told and headed out the door. About fifteen minutes later, Shoota was stepping through the door of the trap. "What's up BM?" He asked his first question. "Please tell me you have a mission for me?" He asked the second. "My trigger finger itching like a motherfucker. And I hope it is them bitch ass Fam niggas."

"Pipe down, little nigga," BM suggested. "We gone handle that shit when the time is right. Trust me, it ain't too many things I would rather be doing than wiping those niggas out. But getting money is one of them. I did all that other shit. But this getting money shit is different, my nigga. You going to have your run though. It is just that by fucking with me, you gone have the guidance to do the shit the right way."

"I ain't know it was a right way to do all this wrong shit." Shoota was a bit confused.

"Exactly. I put all my bodies under while being a broke ass nigga. When you put that money first though, the bodies drop different."

"Okay. Whatever you say. You the boss. So, if we ain't about to slaughter some shit, then what the mission then?"

"Come on. I'ma put you on game in the whip." The two traveled outside and hopped into what they called the trap on wheels. Shoota was the driver while BM occupied the passenger seat. "Park right here," BM ordered. "I know the nigga gone come out in a few. He stays back and forth through this cut making plays." They sat for a few. It was a little less than what BM had expected. "There that nigga goes right there." BM pointed out with his words only.

"This nigga again?" Shoota asked, growing even more confused.

"Yeah. If everything goes the way I have planned in my head, this should be the very last time," BM assured.

"What you need me to do?"

"Beep the horn to get that niggas attention."

Shoota did as he was told. The person who the two YNT members had their attention on, looked in the direction of the sound once they heard the horn. It was Pike. BM noticed him looking in their direction and waved him over towards the car.

Pike sighed. It was unnoticeable to BM. But Pike made his way over to them anyway. Ever since Pike had told his girl Markisha about his suspicion he had on BM, he realized that BM had been acting oddly strange. Now his suspicion was that Markisha had told her sister, Tisha, who had ended up talking to BM about it. With all that in the back of his mind, Pike has been on point more than ever when it came to BM.

"This nigga looks scared as a bitch. Should have never ran his mouth to that bitch. Out of all the niggas in the hood I jacked, he was one of the few that I had spared. Pussy bitch. Every nigga should die for that pillow talking shit. That shit is the closest thing to snitching. Worse than dry snitching if you ask me."

"We can just smoke this nigga right now. The fuck you mean?" Shoota was already clutching his weapon just in case BM changed his mind and gave the green light.

"Shut up, stupid." he said nonchalantly. You ain't hear shit I just said?" BM looked over to his partner with dummy eyes. "Act normal, nigga. Here this fool come." BM rolled his window down a partial so Pike would be able to hear his voice. "You strapped nigga?"

"Duhh..." Pike replied to BM as if he were retarded. "What type of question is that?"

"Alright. Had that shit over than nigga," BM themanded.

"Nigga, what the fuck you think this is? I ain't handing your crazy ass my pistol."

"Why not?" BM asked with the same nonchalant tone he had used with Shoota just a few seconds ago. "What you think we gone rob you or something?" After the question, BM flashed so many bills in the air that it made Pike reconsider his response. "Nigga you know we bring you the most money in the hood. Now give the pistol up or miss this money."

Pike sat there for what seemed like a minute debating with himself whether he should comply with BM's request or not. After a short contemplation, Pike decides to take his chances at getting to the money. Besides, it was his own guilty conscious that was tripping. He only thought that BM was acting weird because he knew that he had done something that was out of character. He knew that pillow talking to a female was not a part of the game. Especially when it came to murder. He had placed all his trust into his woman not to speak to a soul about what he had told her. Knowing that it could be a possibility that she would.

"What, don't you trust me or something nigga?" BM now had that evil ass look on his face that he would have whenever he was up to doing something that would most expected cause someone to end their lives.

"Not looking like that," Pike answered honestly. But I'ma—"

"Nigga get your scary ass in the car," BM ordered.

"Nigga you ain't never known me for being scary," Pike shot back.

"Exactly," BM agreed. "So, what's the switch up for all of a sudden?"

At first, Pike did not reply. Instead, he tried opening the back door of the car. "The door locked, nigga."

"Duhh… Nigga. Give up the tone." Shoota laughed at BM's reply.

Reluctantly, Pike went into his waistband and pulled out the gun. He looked at it as if it would be his last time and handed it over to BM. With one hand, BM grasped the pistol. The other hand was wrapped up in his shirt where he placed the gun as a resting place. *'The things niggas do for money.'* BM thought to himself. Once the gun was safe in his hands, BM unlocked all the doors to the vehicle. "Now, get in," he ordered once more. "I got twenty-four hundred for you. Can you place the order? We need it like right now, right now though." BM made sure he understood the importance of the need for supply.

"Shidd… I got that in the house right now," Pike assured. "You know I live right there. It ain't gone take me nothing but like five minutes to go in there, snatch it up and come back with it."

"You got five minutes." BM assured back.

"Can I get my pistol?"

"Nope. If you want it, then I suggest that you be back within the next five minutes. Come to think about it, your negotiation left you with…" BM took a look at the watch he had brought him as a token to his next level hustle. "Four minutes and thirty seconds." With that, Pike rushed out of the car and jolted towards the apartment where all his drugs and money were held.

"Why you only getting that?" Shoota was trigger man of the team next to BM. But after hanging around his new peers long enough, he had become accustomed to the number enough to know that what BM had just ordered was nowhere near what they had been coping in the past few weeks. "That what we been getting. That ain't even enough to feed the whole team."

"It is enough," BM said with plenty of confidence. "What is up with y'all little niggas keep on questioning a nigga and shit. Like I don't know what the fuck going on?"

"I am saying, BM. If you fall, nigga I fall. So, I am just making sure you stay on your shit."

"Nigga, I am so high on my feet that you ain't even on the ground that I stand on. Now sit back and watch me work." With only forty-two seconds to spare, Pike was rushing back towards the car holding a big bulge in his pocket trying to keep it steady.

"I got that for you," Pike said as he climbed into the car.

This time BM was lacking hard, and Pike was happy as hell that he was. While in the house, Pike had spent an extra thirty seconds climbing the stairs just to go into his stash and grab his .38 Special Revolver 9mm. This time it was tucked into his Timberland boot. He hoped and prayed that BM would not ask if he had grabbed another pistol. He had thanked God so many times within the matter of seconds he was back that BM had not. Pike only wanted his gun with him due to the simple fact that he did not trust BM. In the back of his mind, he really thought that BM was trying to rob and kill him. Now that he had his back up pistol, he felt a lot safer. "You got the money fool?"

"You know I got it, nigga. I just showed you the shit." BM held the money in between the seats as if he were waiting for Pike to take it. When Pike did try at it, BM snatched the money away from Pike's hands. "Nope," he said in a teasing tone. "Same time, fool."

"I can respect that." Pike agreed.

BM and Pike exchanged the money and drugs at the same time as agreed upon.

"It is all here, right? Pike asked. "I'on wanna have to be calling you talking about the money short."

"Nigga have my bread ever been short without me letting you know? Stop bringing up my broke days. Nigga, you know I am getting money out this bitch now, fool."

Shoota got another laugh out of one of BM's replies.

"Alright bet." Pike took the answer for what it was. "Say no more."

BM did just that. Well, that was until he noticed that Pike was taking a second too long to get up out of the car. "Get the fuck out nigga! So, we can get the fuck from down here."

"Already. Just let me know when you need some more, nigga," Pike said. He got out of the car knowing that something just was not right. BM hadn't copped something this little since the first day of the year. He refused to think that now that he had a team, that BM was going backwards. The only thing he could think of was that BM had a trick up his sleeve. Pike would not doubt it for nothing. Since, BM has been pulling a lot a tricks around the hood lately.

"That nigga doesn't even know what he got coming to him," BM said as Shoota pulled the car off and headed back up the hill towards the APT's.

"Shit, neither do I," Shoota talked to himself loud enough for BM to hear.

"All you niggas need to know is that we need to get this shit off ASAP! The sooner this shit is gone, the sooner we can put our plan into motion. We got an eye in the sky that has gone shoot us up the ladder in the game."

Shoota had absolutely no idea what BM was talking about. But just the fact that BM had taken them this far without him knowing every step put him at ease. Shoota had come to a point where he was able to trust BM with his all. No one on earth ever showed him as much as he had seen in his young life.

***

Shy sat in his SUV peeping every move that BM had just made from a distance. Lately, with BM and YNT it has been all hustles. And from what Shy could see, it was just another re-up in play. Regardless, he was on his every move. For a reason unknown to himself, Shy could feel that his next few moves would cause his close attention. As if there was a trick up his sleeves that he was soon ready to reveal. Shy would make sure that he would be right there to watch it all unfold without missing a beat.

Lesson 2.11
Execute The Plan

After a twenty-minute drive, Shawndra had finally reached her destination. The location was Murano Way out in Glen Allen, Virginia, one of the outskirts of Richmond City. The car she drove in was not hers. It was her best friend's, Kadesha. The license plates were not the ones that were registered to the vehicle. They were not registered at all. They were a dummy set of plates. Kadesha produced the idea when Shawndra had called her and told her about what had happened. The rewards of Shawndra having a friend that worked at the DMV was playing into Shawndra's advantage well. They put their heads together to produce the perfect plan. Just by using the license plate numbers, they were able to find out where the person they were looking for lived. And from there, they planned.

Now here Shawndra was parked on the curb right in front of the addressed location.

"Twenty-nine sixteen," Shawndra mumbled to herself as she looked at the piece of paper that held the address on it. She was dressed in all black with a ski mask planted on top of her head like it was a beanie. All she had to do was pull the mask down over her face. She even wore a pair of black gloves to prevent her fingerprints from being traceable. The only debate she held in her head was when would be the time to pull the ski mask down. She was certain that there were cameras everywhere around her. But on the other hand, she did not want to spook the neighbors or her target. It was already bad enough that she had on all black. The gloves could be justified by the weather. In conclusion, she decided to take the safe route rather than to be sorry later.

"Alright, bitch, let us get this shit done so we can get the fuck from around here."

Shawndra pulled the mask over her face before exiting the car. Swiftly, she walked up to the condominium and approached the door. There was a myth that people who lived in safe neighborhoods would leave their car and house doors unlocked. Shawndra tested the myth by Smoothly twisting the knob on the door to see if it was unlocked. It was not which was wise. Only a dickhead would leave their doors unlocked at two o'clock in the morning. Good thing she was not relying on it though. Now that all the guessing was over, she went into her plan, which was to simply knock at the door. She rapped it with her knuckles a few times in a rhythmic beat. No one answered the door as expected. Shawndra was sure that it would be strange for a person to be at someone's door this late at night. Or, early in the morning. However, you decided to look at it. She slightly feared that she would not be able to get into the house through the door. Understanding this would be the hardest part of the mission, she had the easiest way to disguise it, Door Dash. And if that did not work, then she simply planned to shoot the lock off the door until it opened. Other than that, there was no other way to get inside the house. But she refused to leave here without having another body under her belt. She tried knocking again. Still, no answer. She found hope though when a set of lights came on in the living room.

"Who in God's hell has the nerve for knocking at my door this early in the morning?" The man yelled from the other side of the door. "There better be a good explanation for this idiotic act, or whoever you are will get the curse out of your life. I swear by it."

"It is a Door Dash, sir. Your order is here," Shawndra said convincingly.

"Door Dash?" The man asked confused. "I didn't order any fucking Door…"

In the middle of his speech, the man was already unlocking and opening the door. He was so comfortable with his lifestyle that he did not even think to look through the peephole to see who the unknown visitor was, "…Dash." His last word came out in a low tone as his eyes widened from surprise.

That one second of hesitation was all Shawndra needed to push her way through the door.

"Get your bitch ass back!" She ordered as she waved her gun in the man's face. "Now!" She yelled to let him know that she was not playing. As if the all black material she sported and pistol she waved was not enough for him to know. Once the man did as he was told, it gave Shawndra the space she needed to operate with confidence. She did not want him to have a chance in hell at trying to grab the gun. "As a matter of fact, get your ass on the motherfucking floor!"

Shawndra considered removing the mask from over her face. She wanted the man to know exactly where his bad karma was coming from. And the reason for his fate. She thought twice though when she convinced herself that the man had cameras all over his house. Which led her to think of another thing. That was that she needed to hurry up, get the job done, and get as far away from the scene as possible. Besides, when the man was in her presence the first time they officially met, he paid her no mind at all. So little, that he would not even know who the fuck she was anyway.

"Okay. Okay," the man said on the way to his own floor with his hands up in the air. "I will give you whatever it is that you want. Just please do not kill me, please?"

Shawndra swung the pistol towards the man's head and struck him in the back of it. The connection caused him to flop to the floor faster. "I'on need shit from you, pussy. Mr. Mann, is it?" Shawndra asked, already knowing the answer to her own question. "But there is something that I want from you though," she stated.

"Okay, that is fine. Just let me know what it is, and I will make sure you get it." Mr. Mann agreed with Shawndra without even knowing that he had just made a deal with the devil. With the left side of his face flat on the floor, Shawndra placed the tip of the Smith & Wesson M&P 340 Centennial 357 five shot Magnum Revolver to the back of his head. Simultaneously, as he felt the cold steel connect with his skull, a tear had escaped from his eye. The tear crossed the bridge of his nose and fell to the floor. For some reason, he just knew that it was over with for him. But he still tried to bargain his way out of the situation. "Whatever you want. Just let me know what it is, and you can have it."

"I want your soul, pussy." Was all Shawndra said before she pulled the trigger to the pistol. The freed bullet exited the chamber of the gun and entered the brain of Mr. Mann. The contact caused his head to split wide open the way Moses did the Red Sea. Blood splattered everywhere it was able to reach. The floors, Shawndra's shoes, her hands, and even a little on her face. "Thank you, sir. That is it, that's all." Shawndra stood straight up and eyed the lifeless corpse that now laid on the floor in front of her. "Bet you won't be able to step on nobody else's toes from here on out." Before she left the murder scene, she aimed the gun and put the rest of the bullets into the body. It was starting to become a debate on which one was her favorite part. The first shot took the life of her target. Or, dumping the remaining bullets into the dead bodies just for the fuck of it.

Now that the mission was complete, Shawndra hurried out of the condominium and jumped into the getaway car. She made it home in less time than it took her to get to her location. Seventeen minutes later, she was parking the car on the back street of her apartment building. She walked through the backdoor and ripped her clothes off as soon she was in. After putting the clothes into a plastic bag, she walked them to one of the neighbor's trash cans and buried the bag deep into the bottom of the trash can. Afterwards, she hurried back into her apartment so she could get into the shower and wash her body off with steaming hot water, soap, and bleach. Once she was done, she climbed into the bed and snuggled up under Derek hoping not to wake him. She was able to do so just the way she wanted. The thoughts she held in her head were a pleasing nightmare. She saw Mr. Mann's head being burst open repeatedly. The images seemed so real; it was as if they were tangible. Not knowing if this was a good thing, but Shawndra was becoming very accustomed to them. And the most sicken insane way you could imagine; they were even bringing her pleasure.

Lesson 2.12
Take One for The Team

"Foster, are you done with all the tray carts?" The fourth floor sergeant asked E as he was coming down the hallway towards her.

"Yeah," E replied, "I just took the last one down the hallway. You can let me back on the unit until it is time to pick them back up," he advised her more than asked her. "I'ma go ahead and eat on the unit today." Usually, E would wait until all the tiers were done with eating before he ate. The time in between would be used for him to make a few plays and flirt with C.O. Crawford. But since everything he had to sell was gone already, and Crawford was off today, he figured he would just take it in and kick it with the fellows. Other days that Crawford was off, E would still linger in the hallway kicking shit with the other female C. O's. But with the sergeant that was on duty today, he decided to pass. In fact, he always did whenever she works. Every time she was in control of the floor, which was not often, she had to work alone. Unless assistance was highly needed. Other than that, everybody including her coworkers tried their best to stay away from her. Mainly because she had a strong unpleasant smell that made it hard for anyone to want to be around her. In addition to that, she was damn near as big as a house. Taking up all the space everywhere that she went. She was also hideously unattractive. So ugly that it made a person want to vomit whenever they laid eyes on her. That was the very same reason that people rarely looked her way. It did not make it any better that her attitude matched her stench and appearance.

"So, you not going to wait for the extra trays to come back? You know it is chicken patties today." She knew that there was almost no inmate that would pass up on an extra handful of chicken patties. Even if they were not going to eat them, they could always take them back to the unit and sell them, which is what E would certainly do. But today, he did not even have the stomach to wait around for the extras. He had to get away and fast. The odor of her body burnt up his nose. So much so, that he could die from the amount of time that he was holding his breath.

"Naw, I am good. My stomach hurt. Think I must use the bathroom for real." He told the God's truth. After the statement he had just made, E started to make his way down the hallway towards his tier. Before he could fully get away, he was stopped by the sergeant's words.

"Wait," she said with a hint of desperation in her tone. "I'm not done with you."

The statement caused E to grow a little nervous. "There is something I need from you. Go into the conference room and wait for me there," she ordered.

E was lost in his thoughts and stuck between listening to the sergeant's order or bucking the system. Being that he had so much to lose, he did as he was told.

About five long minutes went by as he waited to see what was about to happen. Every minute that passed by, hoped, and prayed that this funky bitch was not on to his operation and had a plan to bust him. Soon he found out what this was exactly all about.

"So," Sergent said as she opens the door and entered the room. "You really think that you are so smart that you push drugs into this jail right up under everyone's nose and no one will know nothing about what you have going on in here?" She closed the door with the automatic lock behind her.

"Well, I am here to tell you that you are wrong. I know way more than what you think I know, sweety." Every word she spoke was matched with her eyes that were locked into E's. "I could really be a bitch and shut the whole thing down, get street charges put on you, and even get the person that is bringing you the shit in fired and even arrested. But instead, I am going to tell you what I want. And after I give you these two options, I'ma leave up to you to figure out which one you want to give me. Now, here is what I want, for you either to put me in on the percentage of your cut, or that dick."

The last word that came out of the sergeant's mouth felt like a screwdriver being stuck in his ear, busting up the beats to his ear drum. It was horrifying. "What?" Was all E was able to utter.

"You heard me. Now choose. Before I choose for you. I already know which one I want. I am just trying to make it easier on you."

Although E was making plenty of money, he refused to bring her in on his hustle. It was just too risky. For one, he would run the risk of getting caught up by making a hot transaction. The system that he and Crawford had created was foolproof. But this bitch was thirsty, and E had a strong feeling that it was not for money. For two, E did not want to put Crawford at jeopardy by making her hot because this bitch wanted to be an asshole and dig into their scheme. Keep in mind, the snitch had already tipped the jail off that Crawford was allegedly working with E by bringing drugs into the jail for him. Other than his words, which still were not enough, that is the only proof they had. You ever heard the phrase, 'Taking one for the team?' That is exactly what E felt like he had to do.

"So, what we supposed to do this in here?" He could not believe that the words had rolled off his tongue. "You know it's cameras and windows in this room, right?"

"I know. Go into the staff bathroom. It is unlocked. Wait for me for a few minutes and I'ma be right behind you."

E did as he was told. He stood with his back against the sink facing the door dreading the moment that it would finally open. His mind raced to a way that he could think his way out of this situation. He thought about blackmail. But how could he be the one to claim blackmail when he was the one pushing drugs all through the entire jail. As soon as he thought about just walking out of the bathroom, the door opened. A bead of sweat rolled down his face as he immediately grew nervous. So much so, he nearly had a heart attack. On the outside though, his demeanor was calm and collected.

The sergeant walked through the door and closed it behind herself. She stared at E with lustful eyes that was anything but sexy. She dropped to her knees faster than a praying Muslim. "It's been so long since I sucked some dick." Were the only words she expressed as she ripped E's buttoned up jumper loose. Next, she took hold of his limp dick and stuffed it in her mouth as if it was a chili cheese hotdog. It was too hard for E to watch. So, instead he closed his eyes and replaced the image with Crawford instead. She was someone for which he had longed. Someone he wanted to have sex with so bad and could not wait for that moment to come. He pictured her sucking up his dick like a Rose sex toy instead of this fat, black rapist bitch. Technically that is what this was, rape. The thought of Crawford, along with the fact that the sergeant honestly was a pro at sucking dick, caused his manhood below to eventually rise.

Once she was finish sucking up his dick like a slushy, the sergeant stood up and turned around. Next thing E knew, he heard her belt buckle unloosing. Then, her pants came down. He did not even think about looking at her naked exposed body. He already knew it would sicken him to his stomach. She bent over and reached back to get another hand full of his manhood. Being that it was already hard, along with the fact that her pussy was already wet, she easily guided the tip of his dick to the opening of her pussy. She moaned as she rubbed his dickhead up and down over her pussy lips. It felt so good to her. It was a feeling that was damn near foreign. That is how long it has been since she has had some real dick in her life. The hole was so tight, that E could have sworn that she was a virgin. The sergeant braced herself in preparation of the dick entering her. It was a tight squeeze, but the moistness allowed the pain to feel a little closer to pleasure. In his mind, E could not even cap, it was some of the best pussy he ever had. Even though he disagreed with it, his dick was loving the feeling. That helped him just go with the flow a lot more.

Before he knew it, the torturing pleasure was over with. The sergeant was creaming out of her pussy as she had an orgasm all over his dick. The shit felt so good to her that she nearly buckled to her knees. Once her lust was fulfilled, she felt slightly embarrassed from the act of sin she had just committed. Suddenly in a rush, she pulled her pants up. Before they were all the up, she stopped. Leaving her dimpled ass cheek's hanging over her pants.

"You good?" she asked. Basically, checking to see if E wanted to get his nut in or not.

"Naw," he replied. "I'm good." He denied the offer and planned to finish the rest off in the cell alone. From there, E snapped the buttons on his jumpers and hauled ass out of the bathroom. As he entered the tier, Flex could tell that something just was not right with him. Flex gave E a look that he already knew what it meant. "Brah, you would not believe what the fuck just happened to me. I will put you on game when we lock down. I need the cell right now though,"

Flex laughed a little. He knew that whatever had just happened was something crazy. He just could not figure out exactly what it was. He had the right idea right off hand. But thought against it because it seemed a little too farfetched. However, he learned to never underestimate the young nigga that he had become close with. He had surprised him every time he thought less of him.

***

Mac sat quietly with his legs crossed Indian style, eyes closed, and palms faced up in his lap. There were over three dozen people in front him as he sat in the far back of the room. The name of the place was Richmond City Yoga. Days before entering the meditation session, Mac had done his homework as usual. To his surprise, this was one of the top-rated yoga/meditations spas. Not only in the VCU area, but in the entire City of Richmond. The last forty minutes was a great challenge for him. He has been sitting in this position the entire time. In his normal fashion, he arrived a few minutes earlier, hoping to get a chance to get closer to his target. But so was every other person there that showed up a little bit earlier. For the first twenty minutes of the session, Mac was forced to participate in yoga exercises that would get them ready for the meditation that they were currently in. As embarrassed as Mac was, he still went through with the stretches. He was willing to do whatever it was that he had to do to get close to his target.

"Anddd… let it go! All the pain, hurt, disappointment let it all be erased as if it never happened. It is no longer something that can harm you. Nothing can stop you from ascending through your charkas. Before you release it all, take a very deep breath and let it out slowly. As you do so, let all the problems out with the breath that you breathe. Now, open your eyes, and live through your existence."

On her instructions, everyone in the room, including Mac, opened their eyes and did as they were told as best they could. "And ladies and gentlemen, that'll be the class for the day." On cue, everyone in the room stood on their feet, getting up off the ground slowly. Mac, being a new beginner, had to take his time before getting up off the floor. He stretched his legs attempting to wake them up from the deep sleep that they were in. As he gave his legs time to recuperate, Mac sat and watched how the people flocked to their leader. He noticed that she was a natural. Her leadership was effortless. Yet, genuine.

About a good ten minutes later, Mac found himself climbing to his feet. By now, a high percentage of the group had left the building. Apart from one or two.

"First time, huh?"

Mac was surprised when he looked up to find the instructor staring directly at him. They made eye contact and he felt how he would if he were looking up at an explosion of fireworks going off in the sky. The feeling was electrifying. Something he only felt when the load came in, or when he made the profits off the load, and sometimes maybe when he busted a nut. But never has he felt this feeling the way he was right now. "Hi, I am the facilitator, Leilani Johnson. Welcome to the group. And your name is?" She stood there with her hand stuck out waiting to receive a proper introduction. "Sir?"

But Mac was practically stunned. On his worst day, you would never catch him so hesitant and paused. Guess you can call it the power of a powerful woman. He thought for sure that he would have to deal with some stuck-up snob bitch, who he would have to have to tear down to build back up. But boy was he surprised.

"Excuse me. My Pardon. It is an honor to meet you," Mac said, coming down to earth in a timely matter. He gripped her hand with his right and soothed the back of her hand with his left. Afterwards, he raised her hand up and leaned in with his head, meeting it at mid-point. With his lips, he placed a light, gentle, and harmless kiss on the place he had soothed a second ago. "It's just that I've never had the pleasure of being in the presence of an angel before." After he fully collected himself, he was able to conduct his manner in his usual fashion. The comment caused Leilani to blush a little. A little was enough to make it visible through her toffee skin complexion. Her cheeks were fluffy and high, like clouds.

Her hair was long and natural. It dropped slightly below her shoulders, which were strong and sturdy. In fact, through her tight workout uniform, you could clearly see that her body was toned and in shape. There was no doubt at all that every muscle in her body was active daily. Well, not all of them. But Mac was anxious to find out now. Which led him to his next thought. "Yeah, this is my first time trying this out," he admitted. "And I must say that until I tried this, I thought that I was in great shape. Now you have me reconsidering it."

She laughed at the honest humor.

"So, from that comment, I'm going to assume that you go to the gym?"

"Correct with the assumption. That is a point for you."

"Oh, so we taking score?" She asked politely. "Didn't know this was a competition."

"That is not the way I was trying to put it. But I am sure it will be an interesting challenge." They paused for a hot second while gazing into each other's eyes.

"Okay Mr...." Leilani stated growing a bit confused. "Excuse me, but I never did get your name."

"Oh, my apologies once more. My name is Brian Macsby. My friends and associates call me Mac though."

"Ohh, Mac?" She asked with a hand over her mouth to cover her light laugh. "Well, that explains it every bit of detail. So, Mac! What are we doing here? Because honestly, I run a tight schedule and as much as I would love to sit around and chit chat, I really must get on to my next obstacle."

"I like that!" Mac expressed with excitement. "A woman with objectives."

"I bet you do, Mac." The sarcasm was evident in Leilani's voice. "You probably like a lot of women, don't you?" Leilani thought she already knew the answer to her question. But was somehow still eager to hear his response.

"Well, I guess this would be a surprise to you. But I really do not have the time to chase women around. And to be truthful, it is such a race to get to me, that I spend most of my time running away from them. You see, I'ma a man with plenty objectives myself."

"Oh, are you?" Leilani asked full of surprise. "I mean I can obviously tell by your demeanor that it is something different about you. But I did not want to get my hopes up." They shared a laugh with each other before giving one another the similar look that they gave each other earlier. "Okay, so here is the real question. What do I have the pleasure of being the one that can hold so much of your attention? Mr. Run Away Man."

Mac chuckled at the new nickname she had just given him. "That was a good one. You up on the score. But no really, I wanted to give this meditation thing a try. It was advised by a friend. So, I Googled one of the best spots in the city, and yours popped up, Sponsored and all. So, I pulled up. And after over a half an hour of hearing your voice and deep contemplating, I figures what the hell. I just couldn't leave the building without having the opportunity of meeting the person who could place my busy mind at ease for once in years. In fact—" Mac words were cut off by the ring tone of his cell phone. He gave the phone one look, and knew he had to take the call. "Excuse me for thirty seconds. Literally, please."

Leilani simply looked at the Apple Watch on her wrist and tapped it twice with her index finger. Mac knew exactly what she was indicating.

"Hello," he answered the call. "Yeah, make it quick. Alright, say no more. I will be there in ten." Mac hung the phone up with six seconds to spare.

"A man of his word. I like that. Look who just scored himself a point."

"Yeah, the last thing I'd hate to do is waste people's time."

"Right, that's big pet peeve for me. Total turn off."

"Same page. Okay, so where was I?" Mac really asked himself aloud trying to get back on track with the conversation with which he was so intrigued. "Oh, right!" He snapped his fingers. "I got a bright idea, since we both have objectives or obstacles, as you call them, to get to. How about we set a date to meet up somewhere to finish off this lovely and remarkably interesting conversation?"

"You mean like a date?"

"I honestly do not do dates. But technically. Yeah, I guess."

"Good, because I have not dated in years. I would not know what to do on a date."

"Well, here is a tip. With me, just be you." Mac went into his shorts pocket and pulled out a handful of business cards and handed one over too Leilani. They were for certain use. "Here is my number. Give me a call or shoot me a text later. Whichever one you prefer. Either way, I will be waiting. For now though, I have business to attend too." Mac spun around, pressed a couple buttons on his phone, placed it too his ear, and headed off as if the last few moments never even existed.

"Nice to meet you," Leilani shouted right before Mac could make it out of the door. "Hope to see you in the next session."

"You will. Promise." Was all Mac said as he exited the building. It amazed Leilani how a man could have that great of an impact upon meeting her, leave with such an impression, and smell so damn good all at the same time. She stood in the middle of the floor twirling the card in between her fingers. She couldn't wait until she would be able to contact him. But she was wise enough not to rush. Besides, she had plenty of things to keep her busy until she was ready to do so. She never gave men a second of her personal time. But for some reason in her gut, she felt that Mac should be an exception. He seemed so honest and upfront. He had traits within him that was rare for men in this age. She felt like it was something great about him and she was curious to figure out what. Little did she know, she had no idea what she was getting herself into.

Lesson 2.13
Stay On Point

YNT were two cars deep coming from down Mechanicsville Turnpike. They had just treated themselves to a couple pairs of shoes each after shopping at their favorite clothing store, DTRL. That was at least one thing they all had in common. Aside from the hunger for money and thirst for power.

"Nigga you copped them old as Jordans," BM teased Tru from the front seat. The other three riders in the car laughed in agreement.

"Shidd... I been wanting these joints since they first came out a few weeks ago," Tru truthfully exposed. "I ain't tripping. These motherfuckers hard as a bitch!" He was excited at his accomplishment. It made him feel so good to possess the shoes, that it really did not matter what anybody else said about his choice.

"Naw, I ain't gone lie," Bank chipped in from the driver seat. "Those bitches is hard." He agreed with Tru.

"Yeah," Shoota said at the top of his joke. "So hard, that you had to buy two pair of them bitches." The joke caused the whole car to break out in laughter. "I been had them bitches. Straight jacked a nigga for the bread three days before they came out. And bought them bitches the next day. I rocked them bitches so much; they crushed now." The laughter grew.

"Exactly why I brought two pairs. Cause these bitches a lock to come back out. And when they do, I will already be ahead of the game." Tru thought he had it all planned out. "Don't you know you about fifteen, stupid. Yo little ass ain't hit your growth spurt yet. Nut sack still empty as a bitch and some more. By the time them shoes come back around, your mother fucking pinky toe be bursting out them bitches." The Young Niggas Turnt were chortling so heavily, that the car damn near shook. Amid cracking up at his own witticism, BM took a long and hard glance in the rearview mirror. What he saw was oddly familiar. It also gave him confirmation of a huge suspicion that he had already held in his mind.

"Ayee." The seriousness in his tone of voice was so evident to the rest that the laughter's disappeared almost immediately. "Pull over at the store right quick," he themanded Bank.

"Alright bet. I need to get me some more Backwoods anyway," Bank said slowing down so he could make sure that he would be able to catch his turn on such a short notice.

"Ayee, naw," BM said. "Y'all niggas stay in the car," he ordered.

Bank pulled up into the store parking lot and parked the car right in front of the store. It was a good thing that it was the store that was in the bottom of Mosby known as Lucky's. "Call the niggas in the back and let them niggas know to be on point."

"Shouldn't have to tell them niggas that," Shoota stated an obvious fact. "But what is going on though, big brah. Put me on game." He was already gripping on his Glock .26 with the thirty-three-shoot magazine extended clip in it.

Ignoring his request to be enlightened on the situation, BM simply commanded, "Shoota, come with me."

"Ight bet." That gave Shoota that feeling he always looked for in each day. The main reason he woke up each morning. Feeling of being able to fuck somebody's life up. If not take their whole life all together. "We got action, jack."

BM climbed out of the passenger side of the car swiftly and walked around another car that had expectantly parked right beside them, which was a dumb move if you were to ask BM. He noticed the car a few times within the past few weeks. The first time he paid it no mind at all. A coincidence is what most people would call it. The second time BM noticed the same the car, he remembered that he had to catch a couple bodies because a couple of flunkies were spying to keep an eye on him. Or so a couple was what he thought at least. So, all the times after that was just down right suspicious to him. It was as if everywhere he went the car had followed. He now he knew it was official. Who had hired the first set of rookies to keep watch on him had found him a new employee. For weeks, matter of fact, a month, they had successfully dug in his business. Well at least his moves. The first thing he thought about was the feds or some type of law enforcement was watching him. But he had not made it that big to have the law on him. At least that is what he concluded. The second thought he had was that them Creighton niggas was out to get him. He had definitely did his fair share of spinning the blocks of Creigton when it came to their hoods beef. But his true thought was that it was the niggas in his circle. But we will just call it an oval because, well you should already know by now. Anyway, his mind raced that the few Creighton niggas he had allowed into his Junior empire had joined only to infiltrate the gang. If so, he would not hesitate to blow the top off all their heads without any assistance. Shit, no matter who was behind the tints of the car windows he was now approaching was bound to lose their brains for even thinking about trying fuck his mission up.

BM took the driver's window and waited there until Shoota was positioned at the other side on the passenger window. He could not wait until whoever was revealed in the car showed their faces. He planned to take one good look at it right before he blew every feature off the face of the nosy

CRIME PAYS 2 | SELF MADE TAY

motherfucker who had nothing better to do than to invade in his invasion. With his gun already in hand, BM tapped the gun on the window twice with the tip of it. The window took a little too long to roll down. It almost made BM uncomfortable until,

"Oh shit!" he said full of excitement but still tried to act as if he kept his composure. "I know this ain't who the fuck I think it is." He was completely stupefied staring at the person that stared right back at him. "Damn, that law of attraction shit really works, huh? Like what are the odds that this nigga would fall right into the palm of my hands? Ayee, Shoota!" BM called over to the other side of the car. "Come hold this side of the car down for me!" He told him. "Your ass ain't going nowhere," he said now addressing the driver of the SUV. BM waited until Shoota was at the driver's side of the car before he went around the other side. "Unlock the door nigga!" He was already pulling on the handle of the passenger door.

Shy sucked his teeth lightly, something he rarely did, and shook his head. He just knew that he had fucked up big time. After all these weeks of sneaking around, following behind these niggas, Shy could not believe that he had finally gotten caught. What he failed to realize though was that he wore himself thin by being around so much. They were bound to make him out one of these days. The thing was that Shy had grown a little too comfortable and confident. Not to take anything away from the fantastic job that he had done. It is just that the odds had run slim. He knew that he would have to get ready to hear an ear full from Keem once he told him about this encounter. And telling him was an absolute must. There was no way he would be able to keep this away from him. Especially, if this intellectually disabled ass nigga decided to get crazy. An all-out war would erupt if even a single hair was plucked off Shy's head. Shy also thought about all the easy money he had made from just sitting around and watching YNT grow and expand in the time that he had. Anxiety felt as if it were about to hit him. Shy thought about hitting the panic button but he was not stupid. He knew enough to know that if BM wanted him dead, then he would have done that by now. Shy smelled something fishy. BM had something up his sleeve and Shy knew it.

Although he had the options to either pull off or grab the gun that was right beside his left thigh, he chose to see just what type of shit BM was on. This could be interesting.

"Get in the backseat." Once the door unlocked BM ordered Shoota.

"Ayee, Ion play that nigga sitting behind me and shit," Shy bargained.

"Look around you, my nigga." BM gestured from the left to the right. "You really do not have much of a choice."

Shy noticed the cars parked on both sides of him were filled with youngins eyeing the encounter. "Ight what maine, what y'all niggas want?" Shy inquired. "I got shit I need to be doing."

"Shit, I cannot tell. You obviously got enough time to follow us around. I noticed you a few weeks back. Honestly thought I was tripping at first. But I thought back to the other nigga that somebody had put on me. Then, I tried to figure out why me. Well, that was before I switched it around and figured why not me? But anyway, you know you playing a risky game, right?"

"Yeah, you heard about what happened to the last two security guards around here?" Shoota mimicked the Friday After Next movie with a light chuckle.

"Nigga I ain't no motherfucking security guard." Shy snapped a little from the offensive and threatening question.

"So, what you doing then, Shy?" BM wanted to know. "Better yet, here's a better question cause it's obvious what you doing. Might as well just keep it real on that topic, my nigga. The real question is though, who sent you?"

Shy say there quiet as ever. No matter what BM threatened to do to him, the one thing it would not do was give his own flesh and blood up. That was not even up for debate.

"Alright, bet. Since I see you ain't trying put a nigga on game, I guess I'ma just must do some assuming." BM gave a few moments of silence just to see if Shy would have anything to say. "Okay, well my first assumption is due to your silence. I'ma must charge your silence to your loyalty. And I'ma assume that the loyalty is due to your brother, which I hope I am right. I'ma keep it real with you because a closed mouth don't get fed. Your brother is the reason you gone make it out this parking lot alive. Fuck the part about me asking who sent you. Cause I feel like I already know.

"I'ma send you out here with another mission. A message. For your brother. Tell that nigga I need to see him as soon as his busy schedule would allow him to pull up on me. Naw fuck that!" BM turnt up just a little. "Tell that nigga he needs to be available for me like yesterday. Make sure you let him know I ain't even on no type of bullshit or none of that. In fact, I got a hell of business proposition that I don't think it would be wise for him to pass up. That is it. That is all." BM used a head nod gesturing for Shoota to hop out of the car with him. His hand was already on the door handle. "Oh yeah," he doubled back right before opening the door. "There is one more thing that I do want you to let that nigga know. Tell his ass if he love his little brother and want to see him again then he'll make sure his ass stop spying on me and my niggas. Hopefully, I will see him soon and will not have to come round Hillside looking for y'all niggas. That is right." BM clarified. "I said, y'all. Cause you is in it now right, Shy?" BM asked a rhetorical question that he thought was humorous as well. "Yeah, you in it," he said answering his own question. "Come on, my nigga." BM referred towards Shoota. "Let us get ready for this nigga. For some reason, BM was highly confident that Keem would reach out to him and hear his business proposal out. He hoped he did. Because he would hate for thing to get ugly over a young nigga just trying to make some money. Even though was a little bit unsure. He still planned to be ready when Keem came. BM was sure that Keem would take offense to him threating his little brother. But it was something BM felt needed to be done for Keem to know that he was serious. He also knew that Keem was a true hustler, far from a hater, and down to help a nigga get ahead in the game. Especially, if he know that he was getting something out if. BM also knew where the main problem would most likely some from. He planned to be prepared for that reason as well and use it to his advantage.

Shy clutched his Glock and placed it in his lap. Even though he knew for sure that he was safe. Wisely, he still did not trust these niggas as far as he could throw them. Remaining in the parking lot, he watched them for what he knew would be his last time as they pulled off and headed up the hill towards the top of Mosby. "Fuck!" he screamed out and pounded his fist on the top the steering wheel. He fucked up big time. And even if Keem would forgive for the mistake, it was something that he would hard on himself about. There was nothing he wanted more than to make Keem recognize him and to be proud of him. So, the fact that he had just failed the mission along with thought of letting Keem down, burned his soul.

Regardless of his feelings, Shy knew that Keem had to be aware of what had just taken place. He refused to leave his brother in the blind for either one more second. "Hey, Siri." Shy called out to his vehicle's Bluetooth speaker. "Call Big Brah."

Through Bluetooth, the phone did as it was told. The sound of a ringing phone was automatically heard through the speakers.

"Yo!" the ringtone was replaced by Keem's voice. "What's up, fool. The hell you on? You good?" Keem was in a good mood, and it fucked Shy up to have to be the one to fuck his day up with shocking news. "Hello! Damn nigga, you there?"

"Yeah bro. Ay look, I got to holla at you ASAP."

"What's wrong, little brah?"

"Not over the phone brah. I need to view you. Got to tell you how Pops and them made me."

"Made you?" Keem asked himself under his breath completely confused. His voice was still loud enough to be heard over the vehicle's speakers though. "What the fuck?" He remained to talk to himself. Shy and Keem had been doing code talk long enough that even when they had to make a code right on the spot that the other would be able to figure it out eventually. Shy kept faith in his brother to unscramble the last sentence he had stated. Until then, he would remain silent giving his brother time enough time to crack the code.

"Oh shit!" It finally came to him. "For real?" He asked but not really looking for an answer. "Damn!" It was mainly because he already knew what was going on. "Ayee look, I ain't even in reach right now. Just go duck off and in the morning I'ma send you the addy to where I want you to meet me at tomorrow." Keem instructed his youngest brother. "And Shy!" His voice was full of authority.

"Yo," Shy simply said.

"Brah, do not go around there once you leave. Whatever just happened, let that shit go. Fall back for the rest of the day and go duck off somewhere. Wait for me to hit you up in the AM so you can pull up on me." Keem's instructions were loud and clear. But he still wanted to make sure. "You hear me?"

"Yeah, I hear you, big brah. Do not trip. I am on it." The disappointment was evident in Shy's voice.

"Ayee."

"Yo."

"You did good. So do not even trip off that shit. To keep it a band, you really did more than what you needed to do.

And do not worry about that nut case. I am handle that shit. You hear me?" Keem wanted to assure his brother. And let him know that he was proud of him without having to say it.

"Yeah nigga! I heard you," Shy said. Even though his tone was hard and seemed harsh. Deep down inside, he was happy as a five-year-old child on its birthday.

"Alright, bet then nigga. See you tomorrow. Love fool."

"Love nigga. In the AM."

Lesson 2.14
Make It Count

The next morning as promised, Shy was waking up to a text message from Keem. The address was unfamiliar to Shy's eyes. But then again, this was Keem we were talking about here, so. But anyway. Shy rose up out the bed and walked to the bathroom to get his hygiene together. Afterwards, he did what he always did next, which was say a morning prayer to his God. This was one of the first mornings in a long time that Shy had woken feeling well rested. The others before now were filled with fatigue. With all that chasing BM and YNT around day and night, sleep in his schedule was exceedingly rare. This morning, for some reason, he felt greater than ever. He had a feeling of optimism that was higher than usual. Shy's optimistic level was already high from the start. So, that should give you an understanding of the level he was at this morning. While eating his breakfast, which was only a couple of waffles and a glass of orange juice, Shy scrolled through his phone looking for something to get into for the day. Once done, he turns on some music and searches through his wardrobe to see what he will be wearing. He decides to keep it simply by throwing on an oatmeal white Smoke Rise Overall overtop of his extra thick thermal top and pants set. His boots were an original pair of wheat Timberlands. And he tops it off with a tan and white varsity jacket.

About a good thirty minutes later, Shy was hopping in his car and turning his favorite rapper on, Lil' Durk. Before pulling off, he put the address into his GPS and prepared to be on his way. After placing the gun in the glove box, and throwing the last of the blunt he was smoking out of the window, he was on his way. It took him a good twenty four minutes to get to wherever his brother was at. It was a parking lot with a single building in the middle of it. Shy jumped out of the SUV and grabbed his phone. He called up Keem and waited to get a response from the other end. "Yo. Yeah. I am here fool, outside."

"Alright nigga, bring your ass to the door. I'ma buzz you in."

"Buzz me in?" Shy asked to himself. "What the fuck is this a fort or some shit." Regardless of his words, Shy still did as he was told. Upon approaching the door, Shy immediately heard a light buzzing sound that was simultaneous with an unlocked door. The door led to a set of stairs which led to the studio. As soon as Shy reached the top and was able to take in the amazing architecture of the building, he was in awe. "Oh shit! Who shit is this, nigga?" Shy asked full of sudden surprise.

"It's mine, nigga," Keem announced to his brother for the first time.

"Why you ain't put me on game about this? This is big." Shy looked around at the gadgets and equipment of the well put together studio. "This shit is lit." He admitted. "Fire."

"I know right." Keem agreed. "So, what is up? What you wanted to holla at me about?" Keem was eager to learn the news of what his brother Shy had to tell him. Unfortunately for him though, Shy was more eager about something else though.

"Aye brah, play a beat for me." Shy made a request to Tone.

"Say no more," Tone simply said. On request, he played a beat from his top ten, but it was the tenth option.

"Oh yeah this shit perfect." Shy was in love with the beat from jump. "I'm about to go in the booth."

"Nigga, stop playing and put me on to the business." Keem was not here for fun and games. Especially when it came to dealing with Shy. He was only here for one current purpose. And that was to let Keem know what had happened with his interaction with BM.

Instead, Shy paid Keem absolutely no mind whatsoever. He figured that shit could wait. Mainly because he was not leaving here until he took care of something first. It was something that he had wanted to do for the longest time. Something he always kept secret. So, secret that he never ever let Keem in on his hidden passion. Shy walked into the spacious booth, found the mic, and pulled the headphones over his ears. "Run that shit back!" He themanded.

Keem flopped down on the couch in disappointment. One of the things he hated to do the most was to waste time. He just knew that Shy on bullshit like every other nigga in the world that thought they could rap. But did not have a skill in the world. So, for the time being, he took a seat on the couch and went through the phone. At least until Shy was done with playing his games.

"Make sure you press record, fool." Shy says right before the beat had played again. Tone did as he was told. The beat replayed and was ready to be recorded. As soon as the beat dropped, Shy went in. "The son of a kingpin/ He thought he was living the dream, why he in the pen then? / now he the king of the pen, cause consequences come with living in sin/ and plus my brother gone, his soul in the wind/ the other in the game, playing to win/ I'm left, to fin on my own again/ my mama's eyes, they'll never dry/ She just stare at the sky, like she hypothesized/ Failed a lot of times, but got another try/ You better make it count, you better make it count nigga/ you better make it count, You better make it count nigga.../

As Shy continues with the verse of his song, Keem was now in more awe than Shy was in when he first walked into the studio. He was amazed at the skill Shy possessed. One he never knew he had. Immediately, he dropped his phone in his lap and stared in full amazement.

Tone spun around in his office chair to the point he was able to face Keem. "Brah," was all he had to say.

Keem knew exactly what he meant. "I know," he replied.

"Why you never said nothing about your brother, fool? We could've been whipping up some magic?"

"I didn't know," Keem admitted intentionally under his breath, but still loud enough for Tone to hear.

"Brah, he the one." Tone gave his honest opinion. "I'm talking about the only one we need type of one," he clarified. Making sure that Keem knew exactly what he meant.

"I'm hip, fool," Keem agreed. You do not even have to say anymore." For the time being, Keem allowed Tone and Shy to do what it was that they did. In the process, he enjoyed the opportunity to watch the magic being made. Until then, he could wait to hear whatever it was that Shy had to tell him. And that was mainly because, not only did Shy have the talent, but he was also speaking words that only he and Keem would only understand to a tee. Every word struck Keem like a lighten bolt. He had absolutely no choice but to feel every bit of it.

Lesson 2.15
Take Your Time

Kabana Rooftop was the place festinate for the date that the two had set over the phone when they did have the time to talk. Mac, being the gentleman he was, was already waiting for Leilani to arrive at the table.

"Well, look at you," she said as she approached the table dressed in an impressive multicolor plaid patchwork button down double lapel trench coat, fashion winter jacket. Underneath she wore a pair of simple stretch jeans and a long sleeve white shirt that fitted her to a tee. "Here all early and stuff. I thought I just knew I was gone get here earlier than you. Yet, here you are, still impressing me with your impressions." Leilani was happy as ever. One of the main reasons she hated to go on dates was that men was so inaccurate with their timing. But here was this Mac, not only on time, but early. She immediately thought back to their first meeting where Mac had stated that he hated wasting time. In conclusion, she overlooked the fact that not only did Mac not waste her time. But he was also willing to waste time of his own just to make sure that he was he was here before. That was the first ultimate sacrifice as far as she was concerned.

"Hey Mac!" She was obviously excited.

Mac stood up to give Leilani a tight and affectionate hug. Something she hadn't had received in a long time from someone outside of the family in what seemed like forever.

"You can just call me Brian from now on, okay?" Mac felt the energy of him wheeling Leilani. But it seemed as if it was in reverse as well. He was already feeling her presence strongly as well.

For the rest of the night, they ate, talked, laughed, and enjoyed their time together. It was so amazing to them. I would be wrong to say that this was something neither of them had ever felt. Truth was they both had. Unfortunately, both of their experiences led to heartbreaks, which is what caused them to give up on love altogether. The food was some of the best. The view was the best in the city. The vibrations were unreal. Even with their past experiences, the energy that they were feeling in this moment could not even compare to their past. There was no other way to describe it other than love. Which neither one of them minded at all. It felt so right that they figured what? Besides, between me and you, no matter how hard they played it off, it was something that they both longed for. In fact, and correct me if I am wrong, but it is something that we all longed for, love. The time went by so fast that the two barely noticed. The time was eleven fifty-five. Five minutes before the restaurant was due to close. "I think they about to kick us up out of here," Leilani stated a good observation.

"Sure do look like that, huh?" Mac asked an even more obvious question. Even the time flew by faster than a jet in the sky, Mac enjoyed every minute of the time he spent with Leilani. With the adding fact that he felt confident that he was able to get into her head and learn more about her. Through it all, he made sure to keep the objective in mind. His plan was to get one step closer to his goal. Instead, it felt like he had accomplished more than a step, which made him even better. Getting business done always made him feel better. The world could be on the brink of its ending and Mac would die chasing a dollar. If he didn't possess the discipline he had, he probably would have put Leilani on game about his team's master plan. He was wise enough to know that now was just not the right timing though.

"You guys ready for the check?" A waiter walked to the table and asked. "We'll be closing real soon."

"Yeah, you bring it over if you don't have it with you already," Mac said to the beautiful young lady.

"Actually, I do," she said, confused as to who give the check to. The waiter waived it in between Leilani and Mac.

"I'll take that," Mac said with humble pride. He paid for it in cash and left an extremely healthy tip while doing so. "Thank you for your service tonight. It was great. You deserve a raise. Have a good night."

"Thank you so much." The tip caused the tanned Caucasian woman to blush with glee. "I appreciate it so much. Thank you for choosing us. And I hope the two of you enjoy the rest of your night.

"Same to you. Thank you as well." The pair returned the kindness. Mac stood up and walked over to Leilani's side of the table. He used his strong muscles to pull the chair out from under the table with her sitting in it. "Time for us to get up out here. Before they call somebody to escort us out. I will walk you down to your car.

Leilani giggled with a blush. Not just at Mac's words. But also at the fact that he was able to move her with what seemed like little or no effort. To say that she was feeling Mac was an understatement. She was feeling him so much that I could not say it enough. It has been a long time since she has felt a man the way she was feeling about Mac. Even then, those feelings were nowhere near compared to the way she was feeling right now. It brought to mind just how much she really wasn't ready the night to end. Not only her, but her soul longed to be with Mac every second of the day. The feeling was unusual. So much that it was so close to being scary.

"Alright, let's get up out of here." Leilani could not ignore the fact that Mac had just pulled out a wad of cash in all blue faced hundreds. Her thoughts were not negative. But she did wonder what he did or where he got that type of money. She was wise enough to know that if he had that much in his pocket, then she could only imagine what his bank account looked like.

It was what seemed like a long ride down the elevator. But that was only because it was awkward between the two of them.

"So," Mac broke the silence. "What plans do you have for tomorrow?"

"Oh, the usual," she replied. At that moment, she realized just how tired of the usual she was becoming. And the crazy thing was that she did not know where it was coming from. Or that is one of the only lies she told herself. Because truth be told, she knows. It is just that she did not care. At this moment, she did not care about anything except for one thing. Mac, being who he was, generating the energy that he had, was able to pick up Leilani vibe with ease. "I really—"

"You know, the night doesn't have to end just because the sun, time, and restaurant says so." The elevator dinged and the doors opened allowing the passengers access to exit the elevator.

"I was hoping you said that," Leilani said with all honesty. "So, what does a night look like after this wonderful date?" She wanted to know.

"Wonderful, huh?"

"What, you disagree?"

"Nope. I was hoping you said that." Mac took a few steps closer to Leilani. "And to answer your question, it looks like whatever vision you hold in mind." Mac slowly raised his hand his hand towards her face.

"Oh yeah, is that true?" She asked in a low tone of breath. She had to take a deep breath to stop her from releasing the moan she held inside. The soft touch from Mac sent a shot of energy through her body. She looked into his eyes and noticed just how beautiful they were to her. Her body was heating up. Her pussy. As the heat rose, she felt it throb. Something she had not felt in a long time. And might I add, it felt so good to her. After locking eyes for a moment, the two of them drew closer together and were now locking lips. After the lip lock, their tongues were next. Mac's hand slid from her face down to her neck then over her shoulder. With a nice firm grip, he took hold of a handful of her titty. As his hand searched for more of her body, it made its way down to her curvy back and taking a rest on her natural plum ass cheek. They kissed like a broken-up couple that missed each other.

The doors to the elevator opened. The sound of the ding snapped them back into professional mode. "Ladies first." Mac held the door for her so she could get out. Leilani led the way to her car. "So, am I following you or do you want me to follow you?"

Leilani sat with her back on the car. Her emotions were running wild and that was not something that she would usually allow to happen. She was a master at self-control and she felt like now was time to exercise her strength. "You know what?" She started with a question. "As heavy as my emotions are for you right now, this is just something I cannot do right now. It is just not logical." She placed a hand on his chest. "Do not get me wrong, I really like you. Like, a lot! You are everything I have dreamed of in a man. But if you feel the way I feel, then you mind taking your time with me."

"And she scores again," Mac said in a kind of playful tone. It made them share a laugh together.

"What are you taking about now?" She asked.

"A woman with morals, self-respect, and that can control their emotions. Not only are you beautiful and smart but your also dangerous as well."

She laughed a little harder. "Dangerous. Trust me, there is nothing dangerous about me, hunny."

"You might not understand how that much power could be so dangerous. But it is."

"Well, maybe you can teach me one day."

"And maybe I will."

Moments later, they said their goodbyes and ended the night with each other on their minds.

Lesson 2.16
Know When the Time Is Right

"This everything from everybody right? We gone need every dollar for this next score." BM had his team of Young Niggas Turnt in the kitchen of their main trap house. "All that shit I have been talking about us going big is finally about to happen. After this we gone be able to do whatever the fuck we want to do for real." He was collecting money from every member of the team. "This shit about to get lit!" BM was so sure of himself. It was like he had already gotten the word from Keem.

"How you even know if the nigga gone get back with you?" Tru asked a good question.

Most of the bodies in the room paused their motion for a quick few seconds. It was bold of him to ask. But truthfully, it was something that everyone wanted to know. They just did not have the balls to do so.

"Cause, I know he will, nigga. That is how I know. His ass don't have a choice. Because if he don't, all this money mission shit gone go on pause and we gone fuck everybody lives up. If YNT cannot eat, ain't nobody gone eat. And I'ma blow the face off Keem's brother if he don't reach out."

"Now that's what the fuck I'm talking about," of course, no one other than Shoota stated. He already had his gun in hand acting as if he was popping his opp.

"Naw for real, niggas can play with me with they want to. I swear on gang niggas gone—" BM's words were silenced by the ringing of his phone. "I'on know this number. This that fool right now." BM assumed right before picking up the phone. "Yo." Was the way he answered the call. "Oh yeah? Already bet then. See you tomorrow then."

"Ayee!" The person on the other end of the phone yelled out before BM could hang it up.

"What's up?" BM asked curiously.

"Make sure you come by yourself too, little nigga." The person on the other end was Keem. He was serious about the themand he had just made.

"Alright, say no more." BM agreed. Really though, he was not trying to hear none of that shit. He hung the phone up and confirmed the call with his team. "Oh yeah, it is on! I told y'all niggas what the fuck was going on. Y'all niggas gone learn to listen to me, nigga. That is why I am the fucking boss, nigga. I gets shit done."

"Okay, that's what the fuck I'm talking about, big dawg." Bank was full of excitement. Not just for BM, but for himself as well. He knew the higher BM went up the ladder, he would have more room to climb up himself.

"No bullshit," BM replied to Bank. "Now, all we must do is close this motherfucking deal and prove that we deserve a spot in the game with the big dawgs. Alright look let us get all this money in these bags. I'ma pay somebody to count it up for us. So, we can know exactly how much we are working with. If it is enough, we will be able to split the bread up and put something in our pockets."

"If it is, that will be good. But for though, I think some of these niggas grind better being broke," Bank mentioned a true fact. But his peers wasn't too happy about the comment he made.

"Now why the fuck would you say some bullshit like that?" Pickle asked in confusion.

"Nigga I'ma get money regardless," Drip said.

"Will y'all niggas shut the fuck up and just put the money in the bags?" Shoota shouted.

"What it look like we doing nigga?" Cee asked.

"Shoota," BM Called out once all the money was in the bags. "Grab one of them joints and come with me. The rest of y'all niggas chill out and stay out the way until we give y'all the word.

Doing as he was told, Shoota snatched up the bag and followed BM out of the door. They jumped in the car and headed down the hill. The drive was short and quick. They pulled up into Jefferson Townhouses which was literary right down the street from Mosby. If not, part of Mosby. BM climbed out of the car and Shoota followed. He waited on BM's side like a loyal dog.

"Who is it?" Somebody asked from behind the closed door.

"It is me, bitch! Open the door, hoe!" The door opened and Kiora appeared in the doorway.

"Watch out, little nigga," BM said only halfway joking. He pushed his way through the door with Shoota right behind him.

"BM, what the hell you want now?" Bianca asked, standing in the entrance of the kitchen. "You storming up in this bitch like you pay bills or something, nigga."

"Shidd... after I put y'all on this job I got for y'all, you might well say I pay the bills." As he was talking, BM dropped both bags in the middle of the living room floor. Shoota did the same. "Who the fuck is this little nigga?" He asked looking at the youngin sitting on the couch.

"That's the same shit I was just about to ask." Shoota added.

"Damn, y'all nosey as a bitch," Kiora said with a little blush from slight embarrassment.

"Dead ass," Bianca agreed. "That's our new little friend though."

As soon as BM walked through the door, Lil' One's heart had almost skipped a beat. Not from the feeling of fear though. It was from excitement. It took everything in him not to pull his gun out and blow a hole right in the middle of BM's head. Luckily, he was able to think smarter and pass that. He knew that if he killed BM right here and now, that he would also have to killed both girls and his little peon that followed his every step. A part of him was hoping that BM did not recognize who he was and take him out first instead. He knew he was in the clear the moment BM asked who he was and left it at that.

"Where you from little nigga?" Was the first thing that BM asked Lil' One.

While seated Lil' One thought quick on his feet. "Fairfield. But my mama had moved to West End before she died." He was smart enough not to mention his real hood. He knew that it may have set off an alarm giving BM a clue as to who he really was.

"Fuck you doing round here?" Shoota searched for an answer to feed his suspicion.

"He with us!" Kiora quickly jumped to Lil' One's defense.

"Yeah," Bianca added on. "We were trying to chill before y'all busted up in this bitch with that bullshit y'all on."

"The fuck up," Shoota replied with humble disrespect.

"I'on be having to many places to go for real. After my momma got killed by her boyfriend I had to live with my grandma. That is how I ended up around Fairfield. Then she died from that COVID-19 shit. Next thing I know, a nigga ended up killing my cousin and he was the only person I had left out here. Now, I am on the run from social services cause Ion want to be in no group home. So, I just be thuggin' anywhere I could. Trying to get some money so I can take care of myself while staying out the way and shit."

Even though Lil' One's sob story was something he had just made up in his head, it worked good enough to persuade BM.

"Look here, little nigga, even though Ion know you, it's fucked up that you gotta go through all that shit. Especially

CRIME PAYS 2 | SELF MADE TAY

alone. But luckily, you ran into the right nigga. I'ma give you a chance to make you some money and put you on your feet. All you got to do is make it count. But from now on, you with us, YNT."

"YNT?" Lil' One asked confused.

"Young Niggas Turnt!" Shoota expressed excitingly doing the honors.

"Ight bet," Lil' One agreed. If this was a game of chess, Lil' One felt as if he had just made his best move of the whole game so far.

"Now, for y'all." BM shifted his attention towards Bianca and Kiora. "It's time for y'all hoes to get to work." He opened the bags and dumped the money onto the floor making a pile that quickly turned into a mountain. "We need to know the exact count."

"Damn," Bianca stated eyeing the vast amount of money.

"Oh my God," Kiora followed. "Let's get to work bitch!"

***

"And you think that it'll be a good idea to just hand the nigga the work?" Keem did something that he rarely ever did, which was question Mac. They were sitting in top of one of Mac's condominiums having the conversation about the request that BM made. It was the next day after Keem discovered the talent of his brother and Mac discovered what just might be the love of his life. Though he did not jump to conclusions. One thing he was sure of was that he had to make her his business partner at least.

"Yelp," Mac simply agreed but afterwards gave further explanations. "It will give him the opportunity to show us just how much of a fuck up he really is. It will prove that I was right all along. Show him just how hard it is to be a real boss in this game. Once he drop the ball, there's no way he'll be able to ask for a shot that he already blew."

"Yeah, that makes sense, I guess." Keem only halfway agreed. "But that is at the expense that he fails. What if backfires on us? What if the little nigga stands on business and come through? And on the other end, if he don't, that shit gone fuck our numbers up. How much you plan on handing to his ass anyway?"

"We gone give him whatever his money can pay for at regular price. And then throw in a couple extra from there."

"Alright then, bet. I'ma get up with the little nigga and see what is up with him. But I am telling you now, Ion think that this is an innovative idea. I'ma go with it because you the boss. But if this shit goes wrong—"

"There is nothing to worry about. It is a win for us either way it goes. Trust me. Ion think my son is a good chess player as me. Or a matter of fact us. Two heads are better than one. I know you not telling me that he will be able to outthink us both?"

"Naw. We can handle it." The truth was that Keem really didn't feel too comfortable teaming up with Mac to take his son down. Fact of the matter is though that how many choices did he have without taking a risk of fucking up his idea. He felt that it was something that he had to do.

Lesson 2.17

Know The Name Of The Game You're Playing

BM was already sitting in the car at the waiting place the next day waiting on Keem to arrive. As Keem always did, he pulled up fashionable late."

That must be that nigga Keem right there," BM stated to his number one sidekick, Shoota. "Come on! Grab one of the bags." The pair hopped out of the car and scrolled over to the Rover that had just pulled up to the scene.

"This little nigga hardheaded as a bitch," Keem spoke to Mia. "I told this nigga not to bring nobody along with him. And what did he do? Exactly the very same thing I told his ass not to do."

"Just like a child," Mia agreed with her boss.

"Exactly. I cannot believe Mac agreed with this shit. Unlock the doors!" Keem was a little upset. But not too much. Being that he knew he wasn't alone placed him in slight comfort. It may have seemed like an even match, but Keem knowing the shooter that Mia was, knew that they still has the ups on the competition. Shoota and BM climbed into the car and placed the bags on the floor in the backseat.

"Welcome fellows." Keem skipped the bullshit and got straight to business. "I should not have to give you the rundown of the business and its expectations. And even if I did, it ain't gone happen. Y'all little niggas wanted in on the big leagues, so batter up."

BM and Shoota glanced over at each other in the backseat of the car. Both had satisfying grins on their faces.

"So, what y'all holding in the bags?"

"This is a hundred thousand dollars on deck, big dawg. Out the gate, nigga," BM stated with a sense of humble pride.

Keem was so surprised by the remark, it left him speechless. Instead, he looked over at Mia who was already looking at him. They said nothing but the face expressions were worth a thousand words. "Ight, well look then, this the play. I'ma give you four for your bread. And on top of that I'ma throw in an extra two more. But I will be looking for that bread on the backend. So, the next time you ready to make a move, just make sure you got yours and mine. You understand the assignment?"

BM was rubbing his hands together while slowly nodding his head. "Hell yeah I understand, my nigga. Loud and clear. You do not even gotta say no more. A nigga 'bout ready to get to the business. Now if this meeting is concluded, I will like to slide. A nigga got a handful of hungry ass niggas that I got to feed. I am quite sure you can understand that, right?"

"I understand that if you do not have that money right, then it won't even be a need to hit my line. Do you understand?"

"Oh yeah, I understand. I can show you better than what I can tell you though."

So now it was on. BM had finally reached the goal that he would long for. The same goal he had promised his team. He could not wait to see the looks on their faces when he pulled up on them all with something they all had only dreamed of. Now the only thing left to do was to live out their dreams in their reality.

Lesson 2.18
Capitalize

That same night, in the kitchen of one of YNT trap houses was BM and the rest of the members. In addition, was Pike. He was invited by BM as a helping hand. BM never had to whip up his own work before. He had always brought his work already hard. So, all he would have to do was cut up the work, bag it, and hit the block. Therefore, he needed someone who had some type of experience to show him the ropes of the stretch game.

"Where the hell you get this type of work from anyway?" Pike asked while comparing measurements between the two different powders.

"Shidd... a nigga peeped how me and the gang was caking up the dough so fast that it made him want to take a chance on us. He told me to meet up with him. Next thing I knew, nigga was throwing me a half a brick."

Of course, BM lied. Yet, the disinformation was believable to Pike. Not for one second would he wrap his mind around the fact of BM running up enough bands to cop his own four bricks on his own. Getting plugged in with one of, if not the best, connect in the city. That thought was so farfetched that it never even entered Pike's brain. BM though was getting wiser by the day. He knew better than place all his cards on the table at a time he should be playing them close to his chest. BM had a bigger picture in his head behind every stroke of paint that he added to his mental canvas. For now, he would pay close attention to the way Pike whipped the work up. That way, he would be able to cook his own shit up. And from there, teach the youngin in his crew of his choosing the game on how to do it on their own as well. As a way to get Pike to agree to taking his time to teach and whip up BM's work for him, BM promised Pike a nice share of the work that he was putting together.

"Shidd, you gone be copping from me now nigga," BM said boosting with his words and new status.

"I know one thing, y'all better not fuck this shit up," Pike advised. "You got a real chance to really turn this shit up. If you do this shit right, ain't no telling what the nigga might hit you off with. Nigga might pull up with a whole brick or two. Shidd, even more than that. I know one thing, you better not play with that money. A lot of niggas that front this type of work do not play any games on this level."

Pike really did not know just how accurate he was to giving BM the proper advice. Little did he know though, BM was already thinking ahead. So much so, that he figured that he already had this shit in the bag. He had the clientele and the crew. To him, things were coming together just as he planned them to.

Once Pike was done turning the half of brick into a whole, BM had a fiend come through to give it a try. From their reaction, he could tell that they fell in love with it as soon as the smoke of the crack met their lungs. It was on. BM keep the word he gave by handing over a whole ounce of the readymade hard crack cocaine.

"Ight fool, just hit me if you need me the next time. For real though, once I am done with what I got in the cut, I might hit you up to come and holler at you to score. I really want some of that powder though cause that shit is like gold. So, if I do not hit you for the hard, I am gone come and grab some of that soft from you."

"Already," BM confirmed the fact that he was okay with what Pike was saying. They dapped up and BM walked Pike to the door. For a second, BM stood in the hallway and watched as Pike hopped in the car and backed out of the parking space in the parking lot. As soon as he walked back into the apartment and closed the door behind him, BM was on the phone having a quick conversation with someone who was awaiting his call.

"Yeah, fool," BM spoke through the phones receiver. "That nigga on the way right now. Make sure you get that work off his ass too. If you do, the shit yours. It will be extra for what you already gone have once we break this shit down."

"Ight bet," the person on the other end of the phone assured BM. "Say no more, nigga. Let me get off this jack so I can focus on this mission."

Without saying another word, BM was hanging up the phone. He knew that Shoota was the man for the job. He has been itching for a kill. Ever since YNT has been on their paper hunt, the violence for Shoota has slowed down. If no one knew how he felt, if was BM. So, while he had in mind to feed his team, BM knew that different animals had a hunger for different things. Shoota was a baby shark, and his hunger was for the taste of blood. So, that's exactly what BM would feed him.

So now, Shoota sat squatted behind a few trash cans in the cut of an alley in the bottom of Mosby Court Projects. His next few moves were already planned out. BM and him had went over them maybe a few times too many. Just as Shoota was beginning to grow a little impatient, he could hear loud music thudding through the drums of his ear as the 2010 Dodge Charger Base covered in all black charging his way. They parked and Pike hopped out, publicized as ever. As if he had just hit the lottery or something. Truth was, he had the slightest idea what that nigga BM had stumbled across, but he was damn sure happy that he was able to ride the wave to the shores of the bank. Little did he know, the only ride he was about to be on was a one-way ticket straight to hell.

As he always did, Pike approached the backdoor. Shoota crouched up on him like a tiger in the jungle. Upping the pistol with sharp shooting accuracy, pulling the trigger like the strings of a puppet. Pike never saw it coming. Before he knew it, there was a hole smack dead in the middle of his head. And he could not live a second longer to even find out why. Now there was no telling what he knew. His body was a cadaver before it was able to smack the concrete. Shoota looked down at Pike's now lifeless body and smiled. Right before aiming the pistol once more and dumping more shells into the body.

"Bitch!" Was all he spat before stepping over the dead man and heading off to his escape route.

Lesson 2.19
Take A Chance

"I mean, I do have to admit though. You are quite different from any other man I have ever met before." Destiny had just answered one of Shy's many questions he had asked on his quest to get to know her. "But the true question is, what does that have to do with you being the one for me?" To be honest, Destiny had been convinced long ago prior to their many phone conversations since she had left the city of Richmond that Shy just may be the one she would at least think about taking a chance on. But still though, just as Shy loved to hear how different he was from his peers, she loved to hear even the thought of her having a man to love on. "What does have to do with you being the one for me?"

"See you missing the point," Shy said for clarification. "It is not just that I am the one for you. I feel as if were a perfect match for each other. Because that is what a relationship is right? A union of two people becoming whole. Not just one taking more from the other than their giving. It is balance. And that is what I think about when I think of us. A perfect balance. And Ion know if you heard or not, but when that happens, the two become an unstoppable force as one."

Destiny laughed lightly a little at the elucidation that Shy had just given her.

"Naw, I'm for real." Shy wanted to make that clear as well. "You laughing and shit." He even laughed with her some without taking not one bit of his seriousness away.

"No. I know you are," Destiny confirmed trying to contain her chuckle. "That is what makes it a little funny. The fact that you are dead ass serious. As if you know what the hell you is talking about. Like, it does sound convincing. Some of it I can even vouch for. But boy, you are not playing any games, are you?"

"When something like you comes into a person's life, a nigga cannot play any games. This is what some may call a pivotal moment in one's life."

"Please explain."

"You know I will." She laughed a little more before Shy went on with his meaning. "See I look at it like this. The direction of my life could go a certain way depending on my pursuit of you. It could either begin to go extremely badly or great. Not as in an opportunity, but like a missing piece to the puzzle of my life. Like we were on the paths of each other's destinies for a reason. And I just feel strongly that if we are too shy about it then we both may miss some of the moments that our whole existence lives for."

"Aww… I like how you did that." Destiny's heart was feeling as if it was truly melting from the words of not just Shy's mouth, but from his soul. She could feel that he spoke from the heart with conviction. As if it was not him speaking. But like he was relaying a message personally from his soul that he was supposed to read out to her once he found her on this planet earth. "Okay, so let me ask you this. What do you think will happen, just hypothetically speaking of course, if you are granted a chance to have me as yours and you fuck it up? Say like, treat me badly by cheating, beating, or just fucking my whole life up all together. What do you consider your destiny to be then?" She placed a little emphasis on the word destiny to match his articular word play.

"Oh, that's easy. First of all though, I wouldn't allow that to happen. There is no way in hell I will be able to treat you like that. You are too much of a beautiful soul for anyone to act ugly towards. Besides If I were to do any wrong to you,

I will only be fucking up my own karma and destiny. I'll end up doomed for life because I harmed the biggest blessing I'd received thus far while living. Look shawty, I done already gave you the run down. I will not say my life is all shitty. But it damn sure ain't all good either. My Pops gone for life. My brother gone for life. My other brother is knee deep in the game, I am sure for life. At least until he ends up like my brother or our pops. Being that those are the two main outcomes when living a life like his. Seeing that I do not want that to happen, I pray that he makes this shit count for something and finds a better way for us to make a living. My mom's here. But she has not been my moms since she lost my pops and my brother. Then, Keem stresses her out every day by doing what he does.

"When it comes to you though. When I am in your world, none of that shit matters any more. Not that my family does not matter. But I just stop thinking of all the negatives that float through my mind. You may say a simple sentence that's just everyday speech for you, but it be the very thing I needed to hear to switch up the gears in my mind. You give a nigga something to think about. Something to hope for. You got a weekends worth of glimpses of what my life is like where I'm from. I do not get none of the things you give me down here. I need you in my everyday life. Not just on the weekend.

"And before you even ask, because I know what you thinking. The things I am bringing to the table is priceless. Loyalty in this wicked world of ours. Love when it is cold. Protection. I will clear the way for you to make your path free from any harm, hurt, or danger. And that is just the few things I see us giving straight out the gate. Which is the same things we're all searching for on this earth. From there, we can grow together into our greatest potential. And with the powerful potential that we both have. Ion even see the sky placing limits on our heights." Shy had finally cut the words to his long speech, catching some air for his longs to breathe.

There was a long silent pause on the phone. So quiet that Shy thought for a second that it was just him on the line. "Hello," he had to say checking to see if he was tripping or not.

"I wanna see you." Was Destiny was all able to utter out of her mouth. She could barely believe that she was saying them. But she no longer cared. She felt the same as Shy. And although she did not want to be a fool in love. She did not want to feel like a fool by passing up what could be the love of her life.

Lesson 2.20
Winner Takes All

"So, Mr. Brown all you'll have to do is sign on this line here and another on this one and the house will be all yours," Mr. Warner declared. Derek was in the office of Tim Warner's. The real-estate home flipper that gave him the tour of the house on 31st street in the Churchill area of Richmond, Virginia. He was ready to make the payment and claim the property.

"So, tell me Mr. Warner, what made you change your mind?" Derek was curious to know. While waiting for the answer, he lifted the pen and placed his John Hancock on the two lines that requested his signature.

"Well, to be up front with you Mr. Brown, turns out that Mr. Mann was into some shady business. The guy owed all kinds of people. Hell, even me. But looks like one of the people that he was indebted too was not like me. You know, the patient type. Hey, we can work this out some kind of way type of guy. No. Word was it was the mafia. Poor guy must of ran too many bets than he could handle. Then again, a little birdie tweeted in my ear and said something about the cartel. The man had a drug habit out of this world. It is being said, now that he is dead, that he would take a swing at middle manning a few bricks of cocaine every now and then. The people gave it to him because they knew that he was rolling in the money. Once they got him in debt, it was no turning around. Truth is, I cannot really tell you who took the slime ball out. All I know is that he has gone and now the property is yours. And being that he had already laid the cash down on me before he left in addition to a few dollars that he owes me, I will lower the price from our last meeting a whole ten thousand dollars. You can take that money and use it to invest it in the house. Up the price and sell it for more."

As Mr. Warner was yapping on about the man that Derek had no care for in the world, he thought about the coincidence of the prior circumstances. Kimberly's baby daddy beat him up and then he ends up murdered in cold blood a couple of days later. Then Mr. Mann, practically blindside blackballs him from the first house that he plans to buy. And then this guy ends up dead. Although Mr. Warner was sitting right in his face telling him of ways that he may have heard of Mr. Mann's death, something still just did not sit right with Derek. Was karma that much of a bitch? Or did Derek have a guardian warrior angel protecting him somewhere about which he did not know. Or was it… Naw, he wiped that last thought out of his mind immediately. There was no way in hell that he could put all of this on Shawndra. When did she have the time to do such things? And besides, she surely would not keep those types of secrets from him, right? Well, that is exactly what he thought. So regardless of how much sense it made to blame Shawndra for the murder, Derek just could not do it. Unless he had more proof. But for now, he figured that the best thing for him to do was to count his blessing and focus on this business.

"All man I really appreciate this, Mr. Warner. You really do not know how much this means to me." Derek expressed his gratitude with a handful of grateful words.

"Oh, believe me you Mr. Brown, I understand. I was in a comparable situation when I first began my journey to pursue the freedom of financial support that I built for myself. In fact, my humble beginnings are one of the main reasons I still have an interest in small businesses and home ownership. I cannot stand it when the big guys come along dangling their dollars over every one's head to control people. So, this is my way of giving back. I mean do not get me wrong. You cannot be a giving fool in this market because we all must get our coins. But to be greedy is a sin in my book so I would rather play fair." They sealed the deal with a handshake, said their goodbyes, and Derek was headed back home.

The car ride was absolutely one of the best he had had in years. He felt as if he could achieve anything possible. He was already planning to his next step. How would he renovate the house? Who would he get to do it? How fast could he get it done? At the end, he was happy about the way things had turned out. If it weren't for the greed of Mr. Mann, Derek almost certainly wouldn't have had the extra twenty thousand dollars to spare on the house. Even though that gave him some breathing room to fancy up the place a bit. He knew he would need more money.

Derek pulled up to the house and hopped out feeling like a brand-new man.

"Baby!" He called out to Shawndra excitedly as he walked through the door and closed it behind himself. "Guess what, boo?"

"You did it, babe? You got it done?" He was able to hear Shawndra's voice before she rounded the corner from the kitchen into the living room.

"Hell yeah, I did it, babe! We are about to be on the market!"

Shawndra screamed as the smiles on both of their faces widened. They wrapped each other's arms around one another and embraced the love they wanted to share.

"I am so proud of you. I knew you would," Shawndra expressed right before releasing Derek.

"Guess what though, boo? You ain't gone believe this shit." Derek's mood had changed up as if he had some type of unwelcome news to tell right after giving the best news of his life.

"What?" Shawndra asked, not wanting to hear it. She has done to knock down the obstacles that stood in their way, it would be exhausting to hear that she would have to scheme her way through another.

"You remember the nigga that had outbid us on the house the day we were there to buy it."

"Yeah..."

"How about somebody smoked his ass. That is why Mr. Warner ended up calling to sell me the house. They said it was a mafia hit or the cartel. Some shit like that. Ion know. But I do know that the fool owed some shitload of bread to a lot of people. And since he had already paid for the house, Mr. Warner gave us a ten thousand dollar cut on the deal."

"Oh," Shawndra said dry as a mouth full of cotton. "Fuck him. I ain't like that clown anyway. I am glad they got his ass. Somebody needed to kill that nigga." Her vibration dropped to a lower frequency. Her temperament was cold. So much so, that Derek could feel hate flowing though her aura. Something just was not right. Noticing his vibe, she immediately changed hers up along with the subject. "Anyway, that all sounds like good news to me. Besides, I got a surprise for you in the kitchen."

"Oh yeah, what you got for me?" Derek asked, falling right into her web.

"I'ma give it to you. But first you must close your eyes and allow me to guide you in." As she was talking, she walked around to Derek's backside and covered his eyes with the palms of her hands.

"Okay, I'ma trust you now."

They were already taking slow steps heading towards the kitchen. "Don't let me bump into any walls or nothing."

"I got you, boo." Shawndra chuckled. "You said you trust me, right?"

"You know I do. Why shouldn't I?"

Shawndra ignored the question and yelled "Surprise!" instead while dropping her hands from his eyes. And what a surprise it was. On the kitchen table was a celebration cake with the words 'Congratulations! You did it!' There were also fruits such as grapes, strawberries, and cherries on plates on top of the table. Other items were whip cream, chocolate dip, and other edible ingredients that could be used for whatever you could put your imagination too. There was a full course meal awaiting on the stove for two. Wine bottles and glasses on the countertop that sat next to a brand new lingerie set.

"So, first were going to have dinner over candles right here at home. Play some of our favorite slow jams while we sip a little wine. Next, were going to have some dessert. Do a little dancing if you want too just to have an enjoyable time and celebrate your accomplishment. Then, I'ma put you in a bubble bath to let you relax while I feed you fruits, rub your back, and do whatever else you want or need me to do to you. While your washing up, since I already took a bath and cleaned up, I'ma go put on that new piece over there that I got for you and wait for your sexy ass to come out the tub. And finally, I'ma eat you up like I have been starving all day."

Derek couldn't help but too smile. His manhood grew just from the thought of the events that were about to take place tonight. In the back of his mind though a light bulb did go off as to how did she know that this would happen for her to prepare for such a surprising celebration as this. But he was smart enough to not say a word. It will all come out when it is time. For now, he was just going enjoy the fruits of his labor and capitalize on his opportunity at success.

Lesson 2.21
Everyone Gets a Chance to Shine

A couple of weeks went pass as BM and YNT progressed in their quest to up their hustle. The rise was so fast, they could barely believe it themselves. To make the situation even better was the fact that they had not even begun to dig into the work that they had. Within them two weeks or so, they were just ridding themselves of the first brick that they had whipped up with the assistance of Pike before he was taken out of the game. Even though it was a decent number of members in YNT, they all were surprised to have come close to moving a brick in a little over a half a month. Guess it was safe to say that things were going exactly the way BM had told them they would.

The spotlight was theirs to shine in. The members pulled their shiny rental cars from the top of the hill down to Redd Street just to park and hop out to make sure they were seen by the whole hood. Not only had their cars and wardrobe upgraded, but their jewelry was as well. Fuck the hood. BM felt as if he was on top of the world. In a sense, he was. That was if it was his world we were referring to. "I told y'all niggas we were gone shine on these niggas," he bragged a little for the sake of his own ego.

"I never doubted you from the jump, big dawg," Shoota expressed full of excitement.

"Naw for real though," Bank added in. "I was hoping you came through, nigga. I was trying to shine like a tree on

Christmas." He was dapping up Drip as he spoke. The success of the money was bringing the team together closer than ever. They were feeling unstoppable and were not willing to give this feeling up for anybody.

From out of nowhere, three vehicles were pulling up to the same curbs of the block that YNT hugged. When the occupants of the car revealed themselves, everyone could see that it was Da Fam.

"Here go these niggas," Bank uttered. Calling himself breaking the news to his crew that they could already see for themselves already.

"Shidd... I was about to say the same thing," Maine spoke on behalf of his fam. "What? Y'all niggas do not want us to stand in our own hood on our own block? But it is cool for these opp ass niggas to sit out here, huh?"

"No bullshit though," Maine's cousin Smooth included. "I know y'all niggas don't think y'all running shit now just cause y'all getting a little money and shit."

"We been getting money," BM defended before adding on. "Niggas just leveled up on that. What, you cannot oversee the fact that you ain't the only one that can make shit happen? Thought you was gone be able to cancel niggas out or some? I told you we were coming. Ain't my fault you ain't want to believe."

"This ain't even the half of it to keep it a band," Pickle announced while dapping up Tru showing that it was some type of unity between the hoodlums from different sections. "Niggas just getting they foot through the mother fucking door."

"Dead ass though. Wait until we bust that bitch open. Niggas really gone be mad then," Drip commented in a slightly joking tone but could not have been more serious than a bomb threat.

"I ain't tripping. This shit ain't gone last long. It never does. I see niggas rise and fall all the time. Have a little run, running it up, before falling right back on they asses." Maine was sure of it. So much so, that he would even make it happen himself if he had too.

"Ain't nobody stopping us," BM assured. "It is a waste of time to even think like that. In fact, if you was smart, you'd use your thinking to find a way to hop on this boat. So y'all niggas can ride this wave with us. It is enough room for y'all niggas if any of y'all wanna jump ship. Cause whoever ain't on this bitch with us, they ass getting straight washed up. Believe that."

"Nigga ain't nobody trying to hear that shit y'all niggas talking. Like I said that shit gone fold eventually," Maine repeated himself.

"Yeah, okay. We gon' see." Shoota, who was not the one to do too much talking finally spoke up.

"Yeah, we are!" Smooth clutched on to his weapon resting underneath his shirt as he spoke.

"Aye, look brah, you ain't gone be reaching for that tool too many times and think a nigga gone keep letting that shit slide."

"Or what, nigga?" Glock jumped in defending his younger brother. At that point, Shoota was done with the tough guy talk. He could give a damn about what BM had to say about his next move, he will just have to deal with that later. But for now, with quickness, he pulled his own gun out and upped it. At this point, he was not even thinking anymore. With excessive force, Shoota squeezed on the trigger multiple times sending shoots towards his opps. The flying bullets caused them all to duck and hide. It was not long before they were extracting weapons of their own and returning fire towards YNT. To the members in YNT's surprise, Lil' One was the main person going hard next to Shoota. The team was all questioning adding him to the team without knowing much about him. They wondered if it was a wise move to make. Was not sure if he had what it took to hold the gang down. They all knew now. He slung his iron as if he had a major point to prove. Or as if he were in a do or die situation and refused to die. Eventually, at least two out of the many bullets he released from his gun had struck one of his targets. The mark tumbled and did his best to run off for safety. The shootout quickly turned the projects into a war zone. Nobody was safe at this point.

Thankfully, it did not last long. Aside from the person that Lil' One laid down, no one else was injured. Especially no innocent bystanders. Before you knew it, both gangs were attempting to escape the scene without catching a bullet in their ass or a pair of cuffs on their wrists. Jumping into their vehicles they were pulling off before the law arrived. The way this altercation ended; you could bet your bottom dollar that this was far from over.

***

Shy's first new single had turned out to be a hit for the city. Niggas were suddenly feeling the vibes of his flow and the truth of his words. He spoke to the streets like a therapist. Giving them another way to cope with the stresses in their everyday lives. Touching their souls like the preaching of an evangelist who leads them all to the enlightenment of consciousness. Even though he was new to the rap scene in Richmond, his talent was not to be denied. The song even caught a few spins on the local radio stations that highlighted local and upcoming talent in the area. With all the hype going on, Keem thought it was the best time to go ahead and pay for Shy a video shoot. Adding the visual to Shy's words. Of course, Shy would not want to shoot his first video anywhere else besides his own hood in Hillside Court. Being quite different from every other rapper dropping bangers in the city, Shy decided to go into his video shoot alone. So much so to the point that he did not even put anyone else on game that he would be shooting the video at this place and time.

Shy had his own ideas for his video, directing the motion himself. All he needed to be done was for the camera man to hold the equipment and press record. He started from the back of the projects on Rosecrest Avenue sitting on the short brick wall.

"Alright, I'm ready whenever you are," Shy spoke. The camera man replied with a simple nod letting him know that the camera was rolling. The music began to play in the background and from there Shy started to rap along with his own song. "The son of a kingpin, he thought he was living the dream/ Why he in the pin then? Now he the king of the pen/ Cause consequences come with living in sin, and plus my brother gone his soul in the wind/ The other in the game playing to win/ I'm left to fend on my own again, my momma's eyes they'll never dry/ She just stare at the sky like she hypothesized, failed a lot of times but got another try/You better make it count, you better make it count nigga/ You better make it count, you better make it count nigga/ You better make it count, you better make it count nigga/ You better make it count nigga, You better make it count/"

In the middle of Shy reciting the hook to his song, he rose to his feet and began to take slow and steady steps towards the camera. As he did so, the camera took steps in reverse shifting the camera to different angles giving the pop to the video. Shy was heading down the street by the time his first verse had begun. "I'm gone take a shot at it, long live Wild Boy/ That nigga was raw, and he had a bad habit/ Knocking niggas tops off, and throw 'em in holes/ Yeah, he use to jack rabbits/ Catch a nigga dosed, Leave a nigga froze/ Knowing he on go, Only God knows/ Why they wanna to get exposed, Niggas just kept snatching/ Until a sunny day had turned tragic, My brother had finally met his match/ And he ain't even fucking get a chance, to wipe his hands or make amends/ Nigga took 'em out the game, before my boy could even become a man/I'm like got damn, what make matters even worse/While he in a hearse, my dad sitting in the can/Tryna pray and plan for another chance, that he couldn't grab with a hundred hands/And with all that being said, it forced big brah to step up and take a stand/He like hold it down, I'ma take this gram and flip this bitch into a hundred bands/Momma couldn't stand it, and that shit is exactly what made me…/

"The son a king pin, he thought he was living the dream/Why he in the pen then? Now he the king of the pen/…"

What started off as one or two people hopping into the video quickly led into a few. Shy did not mind or cared. He was so wrapped up in the emotions of his words he just kept doing his thing. Using the growing crowd as motivation to turn up the dial of his turnt meter. Before he could even realize it, it seemed as if damn near the whole entire projects was out there stepping with him up the street. Most of all of them knew the words to the song. And if they did not that damn sure did not stop them from turning up with the rest of the crowd. Which was a blended mix via young, old, men, ladies, hustlers, robbers, fiends, bums, real live gangsters, and even down to your everyday working average joes. They shot the second verse in the same scene followed by the hook once again. Finding themselves at the other end of Rosecrest Avenue nearing Bruce Street. The second scene was shot with the song being played all the way from the beginning and Shy allowing the hood to take up most of the camera time. Afterwards, he tried to stall time for a little bit and wait for Keem's arrival. He was supposed to have been there a good while ago. Shy wanted to get Keem in at least one scene before the video shoot was over. And it was mutual on the other end. Although Shy was thinking morale support, Keem was looking at it from a more of a business supportive standpoint.

Perfectly late as he usually was, Keem pulled up in a 2023 BMW XM Label red with black and red rims rolling in between its tires. Ironically, the song he pulled up playing was of course the very first one from his label. "Okay, I see the little nigga brought the hood out!" Keem shouted as he hopped out of the SUV.

"Ayee naw," The camera man who was initially the director stopped publicized for a minute. "I need to get that on camera," he said to Keem. "Roll out and pull up the exact same way you just did. When he steps out the car, Shy you can walk up to him. Y'all do whatever it is y'all gone do. And the rest of y'all just do y'all like y'all been doing. Y'all doing great."

Keem, Shy, and the whole of Hillside that was out there agreed with the idea of the director. Keem set it off by pulling up twice as loud, and twice as slow as he originally did. This time, instead of stepping out, he hopped. The height of the SUV makes the exit of the vehicle even a little sweeter. Shy slyly walked up to Keem. They did their brothers only handshake once they met one other before Shy acknowledged the camera and gave his attention to the viewers. Keem, on the other hand, placed most of his attention on himself instead. Checking the iced-out jewelry that froze him. Along with the blue and grey Armani Exchange sweat suit and shoes to match. Every now and again he will engage with Shy by tapping him on his chest, publicizing him up, or wrapping his arm around Shy's neck resting it on his shoulders. And, doing everything that a nigga would do while being filmed in a rap video. All except for one thing. Not once did Keem nor Shy pull out a single dollar from the stacks of cash that they held in their pockets. Shy just was not the type to gloat at all. And Keem knew better along with the fact that he had nothing to prove when it came to the money. Everyone present knew that he was the money man. And for those that were about to see him for the first time by watching the video, if they did not know, it would not be hard for them to see the image through the visual. Either way it went, he would much rather have his money and themanding demeanor to show for itself. Once the cue was given by the director, the crowd of people mobbed around Shy, Keem, and the car repping their respected hood as they should.

"Ight, that is perfect. Everybody did great!" The director screamed over the music once the shot was over. "Let us get one more take of everybody just doing their thing. Let us act like it is just a normal day out here in the field. After we get this last shot, it will be a wrap."

They finished the recording leaving the scene a loud buzz about how good Shy was at rapping and how lit they had the hood at this moment. It was not every day that the projects were able to lay their eyes on Keem. Yet alone in his presence. But as they all should have expected, that did not last long.

"Ight lil' brah, I gotta roll out. Go handle some business and shit like that. You know how that shit goes. I am proud of you though, fool. Make sure you find time to get up in that studio, nigga. Keep coming with that hot shit. That motherfucker yours, nigga. Take advantage of it." They dapped up by doing their handshake.

"Nigga was you listening to the words of the songs?" Shy asked with a drop of sarcasm. "You better bet I'ma make this shit count. I love you though, fool. Make sure you focused out here in these streets."

"You already know how I am moving. Make sure you do the same, my nigga," Keem advised before climbing into the driver seat of the vehicle.

"You know the count, my nigga." Shy gave his brother a hand by closing the door behind him. Keem shifted the gear into drive and beeped the horn as he pulled off from the scene. Shy stood in place for a moment watching his brother round the corner to exit the hood. Thoughts roamed through his mind. Despite all the tragedy that the two of them had to deal with in life, he was grateful that they still had each other. It was an awakening feeling, realizing that he had a chance to live out his biggest yet subtle dreams. With his foot now poking through the door, he made a vow to himself that he would put everything he had into making the best out of his situation. He just hoped he would be able to reach his goal before it was too late for Keem. He feared that his fate, as of now, was sealed with the same outcome of their pops or worse, Wild Boy's.

"Damn, niggas shoot a little video and think they the big dog out this bitch suddenly. Nigga everybody out here know your little Shy ass ain't put in no real work for the hood. Shit, your ass barely off the porch. Out here living in your brother's shadow. Two-dimensional ass nigga. Fool ain't even living in 3D."

Shy heard the laughs of a few people before he turned to face the person who had so much hate in his blood that it braved him up enough to go against the grain of the gang. The hater stood on the sidewalk accompanied by his two known sidekicks. A small crowd of other people surrounded them, But Shy was sure they were standing by awaiting to see how this conversation would unfold. Shy knew the person that addressed him with disrespect. And with no coincidence involved at all, in the hood, the nigga was known as the biggest hater in the history of Hillside.

"Shidd, coming from you, Ima take that as a congratulations. And to keep it a band, I am surprised your ass even know the difference from 2 and 3D." Most of the same people that were just laughing at the haters comment, in addition to a few more people, were now laughing at Shy's remark.

"See that is one thing I never liked about your ass. You always thought that you were so much smarter than the of us." The hating nigga that was right around Shy's age expressed one of the many things that he disliked about his secret rival. "But you cannot be that much smarter. Seeing that you are still hanging round here with us and shit. Chasing these dumb ass ghost dreams. What the fuck? This nigga thinks he Meek Mill or some shit? Nigga, this ain't

Philly. Do you know you are in Richmond? Nigga ain't making it from out this bitch. You wanna be a part of us, then your ass gone be stuck just like the rest of us."

"Naw, my nigga. The difference between you and I is that I have sense enough to know that I can be more than my environment. Not only can I outgrow this trap that they locked us in. But I also have the confidence that I am smart enough to teach and carry at least a few hands full of people with me. So, yeah, that is the major difference. You bring people down. I lift them up."

"Nigga, you ain't never did shit for nobody out here for real!" The hating man was getting infuriated. He was far from the one to be great with his words. So, arguing was one of the last things that he would always rather do. On top of the fact that Shy was getting the best of him with his expanded vocabulary. Without even thinking, he was more than ready to take things to the next level, which was far beyond words. Stepping up into Shy's face, the man continued with his insults. Hoping to finally knock Shy off his square of these years.

"You standing right here using all these big fancy words like they mean something to me. Or like we really know what the fuck they mean. Do not nobody give a fuck about that Malcolm King, Martin X shit you trying to kick. At the end of the day, all it boils down to is, what you trying to do nigga?" Right before finishing his last sentence, the hater using both hands, gave Shy a light shove to his chest. It had enough power behind it to cause Shy to stumble off his reverse pivot foot. But he quickly recovered and planted his foot again to stand his ground.

"I think the only one that ain't comprehending what I am saying is your slow ass. Now you if you done talking about this bullshit, I can carry my ass and tend to my fucking business. Cause unlike your worthless ass, some of us got real shit to do in life."

Not taking Shy's word too considerately, the hater pushed Shy twice as hard as the last push, throwing him off both feet this time and quickly whipped out the pistol that was underneath his shirt. "Like I said, nigga! What the fuck is you really trying to do? You already know I ain't with all this talking and shit."

"Damn brah, you gone whip the pistol out on that man though?" A peer of the two shouted out from amongst the crowd. "Nigga out cha trying to get his shit off the ground, and here you go with that hating shit again. Somebody gone punish your ass one day for that shit, watch. And it ain't gone be shit you gone be able to do about it."

The hating nigga lifted the handgun a little waving it as he turned around towards the crowd of people that stood behind him. His intention was to search for the voice of the person who had the nerve to speak up on Shy's behalf. Instead, what he did was cause a slight frenzy as people started to duck and dodge while attempting to run out of the way of the pointing gun.

"Which one of y'all bitch ass niggas said that?" He never received an answer. Because of that, three or four shots that rung throughout the air. Now the frenzy that was just slight a few seconds ago had turned into an uproar. Everybody was running everywhere hoping that they would not be the ones to get struck by a stray bullet in another wild Hillside Court shooting. Thankfully for everyone that were a part of the crowd, that their nosiness did not cause them a bullet to the ass. And that the shooter's aim was only the clouds and not an actual person. They only wanted to clear the crowd and the way he saw things, talking was not going to get the job done.

During the commotion, Shy made a wise move by hopping into his car and getting far away from all the static. It was not that he was afraid of no man. It just made no sense at all for him to up and kill a nigga in front of everyone just to prove a point that was inevitable to happen anyway.

Besides, Shy was presented with one of the best opportunities in his lifetime. His brother was not a big record label. But Shy has seen him turn nothing into something plenty of times. He had faith in his big brother, and he felt that same energy being placed back into him. On top of all that, Shy knew that Keem was very versatile with the things that he could get done.

"Yo," Keem said from the other end of the phone after Shy dialed his number

"Yeah, I gotta holla at you like right now fool."

"Yeah, I heard shit just got crazy. Already, I just fucking left. What happened?"

"Nigga, I need to holla at you like right now." Shy repeated himself indicating just how important the conversation had to be. "Ight bet. Say no more. Get somewhere safe and I'ma hit you up in a few." Keem themanded. He now knew that whatever it was that Shy wanted to tell him was too much to be said over the phone.

Later, that same day they were able to link up and have that conversation. Keem was enraged at the fact that a nigga had the nerve to disrespect not only one of his people, but his blood. He promised Shy that he had nothing to worry about. And that he would most definitely take care of the situation.

Lesson 2.22
Protect Your Crown

"Aye, tonight was fucking lit!" A member of Keem's OGS team spoke loudly while climbing in the car. Keem and most of his OGS entourage were just leaving Club Jungle after a famous guest celebrity appeared to rip his smashing hit on the stage. "What's next on the list, big homie?" He asked Keem.

"You already know how we do, nigga!" Keem responded. "We can tear up the city if niggas want too. This shit is just what the fuck we do." As soon as Keem was finishing his sentence, gunfire begun to ring throughout the air. At first Keem and his team paid the shots no mind at all. Still, they all, if not whipping their pistol out, gripped them in the palm of their hands. That was until they all realized that most of all the shots were being aimed in their direction. The first one to be on point as always was Keem. With his gun in hand, he searched to find out exactly which direction the shots were being fired from. Once he located the location by spotting the spark from the gun muzzle, Keem upped his pistol and prepared to return fire.

"Get the Dracos out the trunk, fool!" Keem yelled, hoping that someone would take heed to his words and follow his directions.

"I'm already on it, boss!" A nigga yelled back. "Mia here, get the other one!" The man tossed the assault rifle to her and started to throw shots out of his immediately. It may surprise you, but Mia was one of the best shooters on the team that they had.

"It's about three of them niggas!" Simon alerted the rest of the team just in case they were unaware.

"Yeah, I peeped that!" Keem shouted back.

Boc! Boc! Boc! He threw three bullets in the direction of one of the intruders with attempts of taking a nigga head clean the fuck off. Not his head, but he did push the nigga shoulder blade back. Causing the shooter to drop his weapon and stumble to the ground. That effect caused the other two shooters to turn up a little more. Not only out of anger, but also due to the survival of their lives. "Any of y'all know any one of these clown ass niggas?" Keem needed to know.

"Never seen them a day in my life, boss!" Mia screamed over the screaming bullets.

"Yeah, that's a negative for me too, boss!" yelled Simon. "Whoever the fuck these niggas is though, it is a must that they ass die tonight! Right here!" Simon was pissed. The anger amplified his energy so high that the words that had currently left his mouth had manifested so quickly that it damn near shocked him. Out of nowhere a body popped from out of the shadows creeping up on one of the men that attempted to take out the members of OGS. With his gun already held high, the man took aimed and eagerly pulled the trigger. The two bullets exited the gun and entered the back of the target's head. The partner of the now deceased ex-shooter was alarmed by the explosion of the pistol that was so close by. He tried to turn around swiftly to aim his gun at the imposer of their ambush. Unfortunately for him though, he was two seconds too late. The killer swung the pistol in the few degrees needed to take aim at the man's head, pulled the trigger two more times, and blew it clean off. The contents of his head were on the ground before his body could even drop.

While the two murders were taking place, Keem used the time to put his focus on whoever the person was that may have just saved his life. It did not take long for him to make the person out though. Once he saw enough of what he needed, he placed his attention on the last remaining attempted murder.

"Nigga get your ass the fuck out of here!" Keem yelled to the person that had just took out the two men. It was Shy. The truth of the situation fucked Keem's head up. He knew that this night would change Shy's whole outlook on life. Hopefully, Keem thought quick, that Shy's recent actions do not fuck his head up to much. He will have to deal with that later though. Because for now, his intention was to hunt down the pretend predator that was just preying on his life before he thought it would be better to try to run for his.

"Mia!" Keem yelled out. "Make sure that nigga get home safe!" He ordered. Mia complied, already knowing what he was getting at. "Y'all niggas get in the car and follow me!" He shouted to the rest. "Hurry the fuck up! We need to catch this bitch ass nigga tonight. Like right now!" Usually, Keem would let his driver push him around in the whip. This moment was a big exception though. Hopping in the driver's seat, he pushed the start button and impatiently waited for the engine to bring the car to life. As soon as it did, he threw the gear into drive. Within seconds, he was pulling the car out of the parking space and pulling out into the chaotic traffic. The streets were in a frenzy. Bad enough that the clubs were letting out causing the streets to be flooded with intoxicated people everywhere. Keem sped off with a murderous vengeance and he peeled the rubber of the tires in pursuit of the all black vehicle that the only survivor of the trio was trying to get away in.

"Somebody ass much of had way too much to drink tonight," Simon said.

"I'on think it is that much drink in the world to get a nigga that drunk to the point that they gone come fuck with us. Whoever the fuck them niggas was had to be on that glass dick or something," Simon's sidekick spoke from the backseat of the car. "Push this bitch, Keem!" Catch up with that pussy!"

"Oh, I'ma get this motherfucker. You do not gotta worry about that. Y'all niggas just be ready to shoot whenever you get a clear shot." Keem was weaving through the traffic swerving in between the cars that threatened to get in his way. "I am curious to find out who in the devil's hell got the nerve and balls to pull some shit like this on a nigga like me. It must be a nigga that do not know who the fuck with which he is dealing."

"No bullshit," Simon agreed. "Ayee, fuck this nigga though. Cause his ass is a dead man. As soon as Keem catches up with his ass. I am trying to be the first nigga to put a bullet in that nigga head for sure. But did I see what the fuck I thought I saw?"

"You took the question right out my head, fool." Simon's right hand was glad that he was not the one that had to bring up the topic that he wanted to talk about so badly. "Cause I know I won't tripping."

"Ain't nobody see shit." Keem cleared up in defense of his little brother.

"No shit on that," Simon replied. "But you know what the fuck I am talking about, boss man. That little nigga just put his feet clean into the dirty waters."

"Yeah, that's definitely what's happening," Keem said.

"How the fuck we gon' go about that?"

"I have no idea right now. I'ma must check the little nigga temperature. See where his mind at and shit. Until then though, I'ma about to take all my anger out on this bitch ass nigga in front of us."

Matter fact, speaking of the little nigga, you think this came from that shit that happened in the projects the other day?" Simon asked a pretty decent enough question for Keem to consider it for a hot second. And then...

"Naw, hell naw," Keem denied. "Those little niggas would not try no shit like this. Ion care how much they hate

159

on a nigga. They ass know to stay in line. I know that motherfucking much."

"I'on know Keem," the backseat passenger disagreed. "You know how these young niggas is these days and time. They act like they don't give a fuck. Like they want to die on some suicide type shit. You know damn well we do not sleep or underestimate no man. Regardless the age or color."

"I guess. We just must get down to the bottom of this shit. Fuck all that speculating shit. I know one thing so far. They are heading South."

"I know these niggas ain't gone be dumb enough to lead us right to where they rest. Yeah, they some young niggas," Simon assumed.

"You know what?" Keem asked in fact. "We need to hurry up and get to this nigga before he tries to lead our ass into a trap or some shit like that. Nigga on the phone right now calling up some extra niggas, putting them on game about what is going down." As soon as the last word of Keem's sentence rolled off his tongue, a speeding car came from a side street crashing into the vehicle that tried to escape Keem and company. The collision caused a loud boom. The car slid violently coming off two wheels, damn near flipping over. The vehicle that ignited the crash slowly came to a stop off to the side of the intersection. Keem slammed on his brakes urgently trying to avoid becoming a part of the car's collisions. He and his team hopped out of the car and rushed to the vehicles with their guns out and pointing.

"Y'all niggas go and check that out!" Keem themanded as he ran down on the car that they had been chasing moments ago. The car was so damaged that it was damn near impossible to open the door with your bare hands. Therefore, Keem did not even try to do so. Using the butt of the gun, he smashes the remains of the glass that was shattered from the driver's side window. "Who the fuck is this?" He mumbled to himself. He took a better look at the person behind the wheel who was out cold from the intentional accident.

Checking the man's pulse, Keem realized that he still had some type of life breathing through his body. Using his back hand to slap the man across the face, he tried to wake him up. "Who sent you, pussy?" He asked. The man was in so much pain, that all he could do was moan a few mumbling words. "Ayee, boss man!" Simon yelled out from the other car. "I need you to get over here right now!" There was a definite panic in Simon's voice. So strong that Keem was able to notice a shiver in his words. Speeding up his observation, Keem laid his eyes on a chain that rested on the chest of the man. It was a gold 5Th Ward emblem. He swiftly snatched the chain from around his neck before running off toward the other car leaving the man to die behind the driver's wheel.

"What's up, what's wrong?" Keem asked eagerly approaching the vehicle. Once there, Simon and his right hand looked at Keem with sadden puppy eyes. Waiting for the reaction of Keem. "What the fuck?" Keem screamed out once he laid his eyes on Shy in the driver seat. The air bag was beginning to deflate and there was blood everywhere. "I could have sworn I told them to make sure that this nigga was good! For what the fuck is y'all just standing there? Get him in the fucking car, nigga! We must get him to the hospital right fucking now!" The two did what they were told on themand, yanking the car door open and easing Shy out of the car. He was clearly unconscious but very much still alive. At the sight of his brother, Keem grew even more pissed off than he already was. Before he got into the backseat of the car to comfort and keep Shy company, he walked back over to the other car and placed three bullets directly to the face of the one that almost got away. Shortly after, Simon sped away from the scene quickly heading to the hospital.

As Keem held his brother tightly in his arms, he spoke some encouraging words into his ears. Letting him know that he was well cared for and safely kept in his arms.

"Come on, lil' brah."

For the first time in a long time a lone tear had snuck its way from the corner of Keem's eye. "I'll never let you go." He promised as he gripped his brother even tighter. "Do not let go on me now, fool. We been through too much, nigga. I need you out here with me, nigga. You all I got. Think about mama. She already fucked up. She won't be able to take this happening to you like this. You gotta toughen up and I'ma make sure you make through. Just stay with me. I am here." Disappointment flooded Keem's mind. All he had ever wanted to do was to keep his little brother far away from the life that he lived. Now, the more he thought about it, the way his words always contradicted his actions helped him realize just how far along he helped him jump headfirst into this game that he played. Shifting his thoughts to the person who took an attempt on his life, Keem clutched the chain with a tight grip and swore to his soul that he would kill that nigga and anybody else that had anything else to with causing arm to his family, enterprise, and kingdom. He would not die, and even sleep until the deed was done.

Lock Down Publications and Ca$h Presents
Assisted Publishing Packages

BASIC PACKAGE $499 Editing Cover Design Formatting	**UPGRADED PACKAGE** $800 Typing Editing Cover Design Formatting
ADVANCE PACKAGE $1,200 Typing Editing Cover Design Formatting Copyright registration Proofreading Upload book to Amazon	**LDP SUPREME PACKAGE** $1,500 Typing Editing Cover Design Formatting Copyright registration Proofreading Set up Amazon account Upload book to Amazon Advertise on LDP, Amazon and Facebook Page

***Other services available upon request.
Additional charges may apply

Lock Down Publications
P.O. Box 944
Stockbridge, GA 30281-9998
Phone: 470 303-9761

Submission Guideline

Submit the first three chapters of your completed manuscript to ldpsubmissions@gmail.com. In the subject line add **Your Book's Title**. The manuscript must be in a Word Doc file and sent as an attachment. Document should be in Times New Roman, double spaced, and in size 12 font. Also, provide your synopsis and full contact information. If sending multiple submissions, they must each be in a separate email.

Have a story but no way to send it electronically? You can still submit to LDP/Ca$h Presents. Send in the first three chapters, written or typed, of your completed manuscript to:

LDP: Submissions Dept
P.O. Box 944
Stockbridge, GA 30281-9998

DO NOT send original manuscript. Must be a duplicate.
Provide your synopsis and a cover letter containing your full contact information.

Thanks for considering LDP and Ca$h Presents.

NEW RELEASES

BLOODLINE OF A SAVAGE 1&2
THESE VICIOUS STREETS 1&2
RELENTLESS GOON
RELENTLESS GOON 2
BY PRINCE A. TAUHID

THE BUTTERFLY MAFIA 1-3
BY FUMIYA PAYNE

A THUG'S STREET PRINCESS 1&2
BY MEESHA

CITY OF SMOKE 2
BY MOLOTTI

STEPPERS 1,2&3
THE REAL BADDIES OF CHI-RAQ
BY KING RIO

THE LANE 1&2
BY KEN-KEN SPENCE

THUG OF SPADES 1&2
LOVE IN THE TRENCHES 2
CORNER BOYS
BY COREY ROBINSON

TIL DEATH 3
BY ARYANNA

THE BIRTH OF A GANGSTER 4
BY DELMONT PLAYER

PRODUCT OF THE STREETS 1&2
BY DEMOND "MONEY" ANDERSON

NO TIME FOR ERROR
BY KEESE

MONEY HUNGRY DEMONS
BY TRANAY ADAMS

Coming Soon from Lock Down Publications/Ca$h Presents

IF YOU CROSS ME ONCE 6
ANGEL V
By Anthony Fields

IMMA DIE BOUT MINE 5
By Aryanna

A THUGS STREET PRINCESS 3
By Meesha

PRODUCT OF THE STREETS 3
By Demond Money Anderson

CORNER BOYS 2
By Corey Robinson

THE MURDER QUEENS 6&7
By Michael Gallon

CITY OF SMOKE 3
By Molotti

CONFESSIONS OF A DOPE BOY
By Nicholas Lock

THA TAKEOVER
By Keith Chandler

BETRAYAL OF A G 2
By Ray Vinci

CRIME BOSS
By Playa Ray

Available Now

RESTRAINING ORDER 1 & 2
By **CA$H & Coffee**

LOVE KNOWS NO BOUNDARIES 1-3
By **Coffee**

RAISED AS A GOON I, II, III & IV
BRED BY THE SLUMS I, II, III
BLAST FOR ME I & II
ROTTEN TO THE CORE I II III
A BRONX TALE I, II, III
DUFFLE BAG CARTEL I II III IV V VI
HEARTLESS GOON I II III IV V
A SAVAGE DOPEBOY I II
DRUG LORDS I II III
CUTTHROAT MAFIA I II
KING OF THE TRENCHES
By **Ghost**

LAY IT DOWN I & II
LAST OF A DYING BREED I II
BLOOD STAINS OF A SHOTTA I & II III
By **Jamaica**

LOYAL TO THE GAME I II III
LIFE OF SIN I, II III
By **TJ & Jelissa**

IF LOVING HIM IS WRONG…I & II
LOVE ME EVEN WHEN IT HURTS I II III
By **Jelissa**

PUSH IT TO THE LIMIT
By **Bre' Hayes**

BLOODY COMMAS I & II
SKI MASK CARTEL I, II & III
KING OF NEW YORK I II, III IV V
RISE TO POWER I II III
COKE KINGS I II III IV V
BORN HEARTLESS I II III IV
KING OF THE TRAP I II
By **T.J. Edwards**

WHEN THE STREETS CLAP BACK I & II III
THE HEART OF A SAVAGE I II III IV
MONEY MAFIA I II
LOYAL TO THE SOIL I II III
By **Jibril Williams**

A DISTINGUISHED THUG STOLE MY HEART I II & III
LOVE SHOULDN'T HURT I II III IV
RENEGADE BOYS 1-4
PAID IN KARMA 1-3
SAVAGE STORMS 1-3
AN UNFORESEEN LOVE 1-3
BABY, I'M WINTERTIME COLD 1-3
A THUG'S STREET PRINCESS 1&2
By **Meesha**

A GANGSTER'S CODE 1-3
A GANGSTER'S SYN 1-3
THE SAVAGE LIFE 1-3
CHAINED TO THE STREETS 1-3
BLOOD ON THE MONEY 1-3
A GANGSTA'S PAIN 1-3
BEAUTIFUL LIES AND UGLY TRUTHS
CHURCH IN THESE STREETS
By **J-Blunt**

CUM FOR ME 1-8
An LDP Erotica Collaboration

BLOOD OF A BOSS 1-5
SHADOWS OF THE GAME
TRAP BASTARD
By **Askari**

THE STREETS BLEED MURDER 1-3
THE HEART OF A GANGSTA 1-3
By **Jerry Jackson**

WHEN A GOOD GIRL GOES BAD
By **Adrienne**

THE COST OF LOYALTY 1-3
By **Kweli**

BRIDE OF A HUSTLA 1-3
THE FETTI GIRLS 1-3
CORRUPTED BY A GANGSTA 1-4
BLINDED BY HIS LOVE
THE PRICE YOU PAY FOR LOVE 1-3
DOPE GIRL MAGIC 1-3
By **Destiny Skai**

A KINGPIN'S AMBITION
A KINGPIN'S AMBITION II
I MURDER FOR THE DOUGH
By **Ambitious**

TRUE SAVAGE 1-7
DOPE BOY MAGIC 1-3
MIDNIGHT CARTEL 1-3
CITY OF KINGZ 1&2
NIGHTMARE ON SILENT AVE
THE PLUG OF LIL MEXICO 1&2
CLASSIC CITY
By **Chris Green**

A GANGSTER'S REVENGE 1-4
THE BOSS MAN'S DAUGHTERS 1-5
A SAVAGE LOVE 1&2
BAE BELONGS TO ME 1&2
A HUSTLER'S DECEIT 1-3
WHAT BAD BITCHES DO 1-3
SOUL OF A MONSTER 1-3
KILL ZONE
A DOPE BOY'S QUEEN 1-3
TIL DEATH 1-3
IMMA DIE BOUT MINE 1-4
By **Aryanna**

A DOPEBOY'S PRAYER
By **Eddie "Wolf" Lee**

THE KING CARTEL 1-3
By **Frank Gresham**

THESE NIGGAS AIN'T LOYAL 1-3
By **Nikki Tee**

GANGSTA SHYT 1-3
By **CATO**

THE ULTIMATE BETRAYAL
By **Phoenix**

BOSS'N UP 1-3
By **Royal Nicole**

I LOVE YOU TO DEATH
By **Destiny J**

I RIDE FOR MY HITTA
I STILL RIDE FOR MY HITTA
By **Misty Holt**

LOVE & CHASIN' PAPER
By **Qay Crockett**

TO DIE IN VAIN
SINS OF A HUSTLA
By **ASAD**

BROOKLYN HUSTLAZ
By **Boogsy Morina**

BROOKLYN ON LOCK 1 & 2
By **Sonovia**

GANGSTA CITY
By **Teddy Duke**

A DRUG KING AND HIS DIAMOND 1-3
A DOPEMAN'S RICHES
HER MAN, MINE'S TOO 1&2
CASH MONEY HO'S
THE WIFEY I USED TO BE 1&2
PRETTY GIRLS DO NASTY THINGS
By **Nicole Goosby**

LIPSTICK KILLAH 1-3
CRIME OF PASSION 1-3
FRIEND OR FOE 1-3
By **Mimi**

TRAPHOUSE KING 1-3
KINGPIN KILLAZ 1-3
STREET KINGS 1&2
PAID IN BLOOD 1&2
CARTEL KILLAZ 1-3
DOPE GODS 1&2
By **Hood Rich**

THE STREETS ARE CALLING
By **Duquie Wilson**

CRIME PAYS 2 | SELF MADE TAY

STEADY MOBBN' 1-3
THE STREETS STAINED MY SOUL 1-3
By **Marcellus Allen**

WHO SHOT YA 1-3
SON OF A DOPE FIEND 1-4
HEAVEN GOT A GHETTO 1&2
SKI MASK MONEY 1&2
By **Renta**

GORILLAZ IN THE BAY 1-4
TEARS OF A GANGSTA 1/&2
3X KRAZY 1&2
STRAIGHT BEAST MODE 1&2
By **DE'KARI**

TRIGGADALE 1-3
MURDA WAS THE CASE 1-3
By **Elijah R. Freeman**

SLAUGHTER GANG 1-3
RUTHLESS HEART 1-3
By **Willie Slaughter**

GOD BLESS THE TRAPPERS 1-3
THESE SCANDALOUS STREETS 1-3
FEAR MY GANGSTA 1-5
THESE STREETS DON'T LOVE NOBODY 1-2
BURY ME A G 1-5
A GANGSTA'S EMPIRE 1-4
THE DOPEMAN'S BODYGAURD 1&2
THE REALEST KILLAZ 1-3
THE LAST OF THE OGS 1-3
By **Tranay Adams**

MARRIED TO A BOSS 1-3
By **Destiny Skai & Chris Green**

KINGZ OF THE GAME 1-7
CRIME BOSS 1-3
By **Playa Ray**

FUK SHYT
By **Blakk Diamond**

DON'T F#CK WITH MY HEART 1&2
By **Linnea**

ADDICTED TO THE DRAMA 1-3
IN THE ARM OF HIS BOSS
By **Jamila**

LOYALTY AIN'T PROMISED 1&2
By **Keith Williams**

YAYO 1-4
A SHOOTER'S AMBITION 1&2
BRED IN THE GAME
By **S. Allen**

TRAP GOD 1-3
RICH $AVAGE 1-3
MONEY IN THE GRAVE 1-3
CARTEL MONEY
By **Martell Troublesome Bolden**

FOREVER GANGSTA 1&2
GLOCKS ON SATIN SHEETS 1&2
By **Adrian Dulan**

TOE TAGZ 1-4
LEVELS TO THIS SHYT 1&2
IT'S JUST ME AND YOU
By **Ah'Million**

CRIME PAYS 2 | SELF MADE TAY

KINGPIN DREAMS 1-3
RAN OFF ON DA PLUG
By **Paper Boi Rari**

THE STREETS MADE ME 1-3
By **Larry D. Wright**

CONFESSIONS OF A GANGSTA 1-4
CONFESSIONS OF A JACKBOY 1-3
CONFESSIONS OF A HITMAN
By **Nicholas Lock**

I'M NOTHING WITHOUT HIS LOVE
SINS OF A THUG
TO THE THUG I LOVED BEFORE
A GANGSTA SAVED XMAS
IN A HUSTLER I TRUST
By **Monet Dragun**

QUIET MONEY 1-3
THUG LIFE 1-3
EXTENDED CLIP 1&2
A GANGSTA'S PARADISE
By **Trai'Quan**

CAUGHT UP IN THE LIFE 1-3
THE STREETS NEVER LET GO 1-3
By **Robert Baptiste**

NEW TO THE GAME 1-3
MONEY, MURDER & MEMORIES 1-3
By **Malik D. Rice**

CREAM 2-3
THE STREETS WILL TALK
By **Yolanda Moore**

THE STREETS WILL NEVER CLOSE 1-3
By **K'ajji**

LIFE OF A SAVAGE 1-4
A GANGSTA'S QUR'AN 1-4
MURDA SEASON 1-3
GANGLAND CARTEL 1-3
CHI'RAQ GANGSTAS 1-4
KILLERS ON ELM STREET 1-3
JACK BOYZ N DA BRONX 1-3
A DOPEBOY'S DREAM 1-3
JACK BOYS VS DOPE BOYS 1-3
COKE GIRLZ
COKE BOYS
SOSA GANG 1&2
BRONX SAVAGES
BODYMORE KINGPINS
BLOOD OF A GOON
By **Romell Tukes**

CONCRETE KILLA 1-3
VICIOUS LOYALTY 1-3
By **Kingpen**

THE ULTIMATE SACRIFICE 1-6
KHADIFI
IF YOU CROSS ME ONCE 1-3
ANGEL 1-4
IN THE BLINK OF AN EYE
By **Anthony Fields**

THE LIFE OF A HOOD STAR
By **Ca$h & Rashia Wilson**

NIGHTMARES OF A HUSTLA 1-3
BLOOD AND GAMES 1&2
By **King Dream**

GHOST MOB
By **Stilloan Robinson**

CRIME PAYS 2 | SELF MADE TAY

HARD AND RUTHLESS 1&2
MOB TOWN 251
THE BILLIONAIRE BENTLEYS 1-3
REAL G'S MOVE IN SILENCE
By **Von Diesel**

MOB TIES 1-7
SOUL OF A HUSTLER, HEART OF A KILLER 1-3
GORILLAZ IN THE TRENCHES
By **SayNoMore**

BODYMORE MURDERLAND 1-3
THE BIRTH OF A GANGSTER 1-4
By **Delmont Player**

FOR THE LOVE OF A BOSS 1&2
By **C. D. Blue**

KILLA KOUNTY 1-5
By **Khufu**

MOBBED UP 1-4
THE BRICK MAN 1-5
THE COCAINE PRINCESS 1-10
STEPPERS 1-3
SUPER GREMLIN 1-4
By **King Rio**

MONEY GAME 1&2
By **Smoove Dolla**

A GANGSTA'S KARMA 1-4
By **FLAME**

KING OF THE TRENCHES 1-3
By **GHOST & TRANAY ADAMS**

QUEEN OF THE ZOO 1&2
By **Black Migo**

GRIMEY WAYS 1-3
BETRAYAL OF A G
By **Ray Vinci**

XMAS WITH AN ATL SHOOTER
By **Ca$h & Destiny Skai**

KING KILLA 1&2
By **Vincent "Vitto" Holloway**

BETRAYAL OF A THUG 1&2
By **Fre$h**

THE MURDER QUEENS 1-5
By **Michael Gallon**

FOR THE LOVE OF BLOOD 1-4
By **Jamel Mitchell**

HOOD CONSIGLIERE 1&2
NO TIME FOR ERROR
By **Keese**

PROTÉGÉ OF A LEGEND 1&2
LOVE IN THE TRENCHES 1&2
By **Corey Robinson**

THE PLUG'S RUTHLESS DAUGHTER
By **Tony Daniels**

BORN IN THE GRAVE 1-3
CRIME PAYS
By **Self Made Tay**

MOAN IN MY MOUTH
By **XTASY**

CRIME PAYS 2 | SELF MADE TAY

TORN BETWEEN A GANGSTER AND A GENTLEMAN
By **J-BLUNT & Miss Kim**

LOYALTY IS EVERYTHING 1-3
CITY OF SMOKE 1&2
By **Molotti**

HERE TODAY GONE TOMORROW 1&2
By **Fly Rock**

WOMEN LIE MEN LIE 1-4
FIFTY SHADES OF SNOW 1-3
STACK BEFORE YOU SPLURGE
GIRLS FALL LIKE DOMINOES
NAÏVE TO THE STREETS
By **ROY MILLIGAN**

PILLOW PRINCESS
By **S. Hawkins**

THE BUTTERFLY MAFIA 1-3
SALUTE MY SAVAGERY 1&2
By **Fumiya Payne**

THE LANE 1&2
By Ken-Ken Spence

THE PUSSY TRAP 1-5
By **Nene Capri**

DIRTY DNA
By **Blaque**

SANCTIFIED AND HORNY
by **XTASY**

BOOKS BY LDP'S CEO, CA$H

TRUST IN NO MAN
TRUST IN NO MAN 2
TRUST IN NO MAN 3
BONDED BY BLOOD
SHORTY GOT A THUG
THUGS CRY
THUGS CRY 2
THUGS CRY 3
TRUST NO BITCH
TRUST NO BITCH 2
TRUST NO BITCH 3
TIL MY CASKET DROPS
RESTRAINING ORDER
RESTRAINING ORDER 2
IN LOVE WITH A CONVICT
LIFE OF A HOOD STAR
XMAS WITH AN ATL SHOOTER

www.ingramcontent.com/pod-product-compliance
Lightning Source LLC
Chambersburg PA
CBHW070523260626
47161CB00004B/1625